Comanchero Kingdom

'Kill him!'

The fierce command ripped the desert night apart. For young Danny Ketchell, it was the most desperate moment of his life. As he raked his horse with spurs to crash his way headlong into the encircling Comancheros, his six gun roared and enemy rifles snarled back.

Before there could be peace, first there must be blood. . . .

By the same author

One Deadly Summer
The Yuma Sanction
Ride a Godless Lane
Chancy Rides Alone
Helltown Marshal
Colt Heat
Gun Lords of Texas
Always the Guns
By the Gun they Died
The Last Gundown

Comanchero Kingdom

Matt James

© Matt James 2011
First published in Great Britain 2011

ISBN 978-0-7090-9080-9

Robert Hale Limited
Clerkenwell House
Clerkenwell Green
London EC1R 0HT

www.halebooks.com

The right of Matt James to be identified as
author of this work has been asserted by him
in accordance with the Copyright, Designs and
Patents Act 1988

Typeset by
Derek Doyle & Associates, Shaw Heath
Printed and bound in Great Britain by
CPI Antony Rowe, Chippenham and Eastbourne

CHAPTER 1

THE BROTHERS

The sun struck fire from the badge on his chest as Jack Emerson stepped down off the law-office porch. He paused a moment to glance both ways before setting off down the main street of Hudson, squinting against the glare of a hot Texas noon.

Upon gaining the shadowed porch of the Rye Patch Saloon he paused to take a perfunctory look over the town – his town.

For some reason this scorching heat appeared to have less effect than usual upon the siesta-loving Texans that day, for there were any number of citizens to be seen along the boardwalks, while a leisurely stream of vehicles and horsemen moved both ways along Buffalo Street.

The day being Friday, plus the ball to be held that night at the Bella Union, would account for the added activity, he mused.

Continuing on his leisurely patrol he traded nods with all he met, and to a man they responded, every one.

He was tall and lean, Jack Emerson, well-made and straight with a complexion tanned deeply by the Texas sun, hair the colour of new rope.

Folks here thought he appeared younger than his twenty-seven years, and he was certainly the most youthful sheriff Hudson had ever had. Too young, or so many had attested when he first took office two years back. But the critics had been quickly silenced by his achievements. Nowadays, there were any number in the county happy to insist that Emerson was the best damned lawman in the whole Lone Star State.

These were the ones who'd seen behind his quiet and reserved manner to uncover a man of iron determination and ruthless adherence to the letter of the law, despite his easy-seeming ways.

He halted when a passer-by placed a detaining hand on his arm. Bill Dobbs was manager of the Hudson Bank.

'Heading home for chow, Jack?' the banker

asked, swabbing sweat from his forehead with a polka-dot kerchief.

'Uh-huh,' Jack nodded. He liked the portly little banker, a man always unafraid to back up his faith in Hudson with cold cash when required.

'Reckoned you would be,' Hudson grinned. 'If that new bride of yours cooks only half as good as she looks her meals would just have to be a huge improvement on the grub they dish up at the Bella Union.'

'She'll be happy to hear that.'

Emerson was about to move on when he remembered something. 'Say, how are you making out with that call-up for old bank notes, Bill?'

'They're still coming in. We shipped three thousand dollars worth back to the Central Bank last week, but they're still being presented.'

'When do you plan to ship the next lot out?'

'Monday. There'll be a special stage coming through with four bank guards on it. We can't be too careful, y'know. Those notes are still good currency until the Central Bank announces a halt to the call-in.'

'They issued you plenty new bills to trade in for the old stuff, did they?'

'Sure did. All told, we've about twelve thousand dollars in the bank right now.'

Emerson glanced across the street at the solid bulk of the Hudson Bank. It was new, with colonnades in front and gleamed with fresh white paint, yet for some reason he found himself frowning now.

Dobbs read his expression accurately. 'Uh-huh, you're thinking that's a big heap of money to be holding, aren't you, Jack? But there's no call for concern. We've got a strong vault to house it in plus a top sheriff to make sure nothing happens to it.'

Jack accepted the compliment with a grin as Dobbs patted him on the shoulder and headed off to his bank.

The lawman continued on his way to swing down Piñon Street and eventually reached his modest frame house. Pushing through the picket gate, he glanced back the way he'd come. He paused. A man had been standing on the corner of Piñon and Lacey Streets moments before, but wasn't there now.

Hand upon the gate, he waited for the figure to reappear. He'd only caught an oblique glimpse yet felt sure it had been young Danny Ketchell – his wife's brother – who'd appeared to be watching him. He frowned as he continued slowly up the path, vaguely puzzled by the boy's failure to toss him a salute . . . some sign of recognition.

He was still preoccupied when Carmel appeared in the doorway. He quickly smiled, but not convincingly enough, so it seemed.

'I saw that look, Jack Emerson,' she said banteringly. 'Now, what could put such a worried frown on the face of Hudson's fearless peace officer?'

His frown was gone as he bent to kiss her. 'Nothing,' he assured. 'Well, nothing important anyway.'

It was cool in the front room with the shades drawn against the heat. He poured a tumbler of water while his wife brought in the meal and placed it upon a snowy cloth on the big table. She was chatting inconsequentially when she suddenly realized he wasn't listening.

He caught her glance, and said, 'When did you see Danny last, honey?'

'Why, Wednesday, I think. Why, Jack?'

'Just curious, I guess. What's he been doing these days? Got a steady job yet?'

Her seriousness now matched his own. 'No, he didn't mention any job, yet he seemed well.' She drew closer, blue eyes questioning. 'What is it, Jack? Is Danny in trouble? You must tell me. Having one outlaw brother is more than enough. I don't know if I could bear it if Danny. . . .'

Her voice trailed off and he placed his hands on her shoulders.

'There's nothing wrong,' he assured. 'I'm just curious, is all.'

The reality was that the lawman had maintained a keen interest in her younger brother dating back to when he first began dating Carmel. Danny Ketchell was a wild and headstrong boy who'd been in several minor scrapes before Emerson took over as sheriff. He'd taken the youth under his wing, took him hunting and even taught him how to use weapons – for a time. He'd been tutoring him in the clean and draw until suddenly deciding that Danny seemed far too interested in weapons and showed more skill in their use than he felt comfortable with. So he'd suddenly dropped the weapons' training and the boy had grown resentful and distant as a result.

That was some months back now. During that time the gap between them had widened until now the two rarely met, and when they did it was usually just a grunt or a nod to substitute for the old easy friendship.

'Food all ready,' Carmel broke in on his thoughts.

'And I'm double ready for it.' He drew out her chair and bowed. 'After you, Mrs E.'

She sat down smiling and he was drawing out his own chair when the sudden crash of a gunshot from uptown saw him freeze.

For one brief moment husband and wife exchanged stares. Then Emerson was kicking his chair aside to run for the door as that first shot was followed by a wild explosion of six-gun fire mingling with shouts, screams and the sudden drumming of hoofbeats.

'Jack!' Carmel cried, rushing from the room after him. But by the time she'd reached the gallery he had leapt the picket fence to go running off towards the sounds of violence, six-gun in hand now.

Legging it fast along Pinto he glimpsed citizens fleeing south along Buffalo while casting wild glances over their shoulders back in the direction of the bank.

A frenzied fat woman clutching a pair of squawling infants in powerful red arms almost collided with him as he cut around the post office corner. At the same moment, rancher Jett Bucker all but capsized his buckboard as he cornered at twice the safe speed, standing and flaying the wild-eyed team.

'The bank!' the man roared to Jack as he thundered past. 'Bin robbed!'

Two blocks north along Buffalo Jack was greeted by a scene such as this town had never seen. Out front of the Hudson Bank four men with bandannas hiding their faces were flinging bulging pack-saddles across plunging horses and shooting wildly into the sky as they fitted boots to stirrups to mount up.

From a window opposite the bank building, jets of hot gun flame spurted viciously at the bandits and bullets howled and whined along the street, shattering windows and adding to the uproar.

Two bloodied figures lay sprawled upon the bank steps and even as Emerson touched off his first racketing shot, he saw that one of those men was Bill Dobbs.

A masked figure astride a red stallion burst around a corner to rake viciously with spur and go racing away with the others thundering close behind.

With a hoarse curse, Emerson propped and swept Colt up to eye-level. He fixed his sights upon a check-shirted figure, squeezed trigger. The rider flinched as lead bit deep yet kept his seat in the saddle and spurred away, still at headlong speed.

Again the lawman's Colt smoked and this time the fleeing rider rose stiffly in his stirrups, eyes bugging and spine arching in agony as he curved over backwards upon the animal's rump, hung there for racing seconds staring sightlessly at the sky then dropped into the dust and lay still.

Before he could notch another target in his gunsights the robbers were storming out of sight around Finster's Barn with the butter-yellow dust boiling from hammering hoofs billowing behind.

The lawman touched off three fast shots but knew all were wild – then swiftly the robbers were gone from sight with the riderless mount galloping after them.

A breathless moment passed in total silence. Then the first angry citizens, some hefting shotguns and others with smoking side arms in hand erupted from alleys and doorways, while Emerson fingered shells into his hot piece and ran off towards the bank.

The men sprawled upon the bank steps were stirring and moaning, both nursing wounds. The first black-suited figure he identified as the teller, Dick Tolliver, only lightly creased by the look of it. But Dobbs appeared more seriously hurt with blood pouring from a thigh wound and his face ashen.

Jack dropped to one knee at Dobbs's side and went to work, ripping out a shirt sleeve which he then applied as a tourniquet, all in just a handful of seconds. Bad enough but not fatal, was his diagnosis. The slug had gone in high under the shoulder before exiting at the back, leaving a free-bleeding wound which he swiftly staunched.

By this the street was swarming with citizens who gaped in shock as they saw Tolliver toted away. Others clustered around the man Emerson had gunned down, none with pity and most with hate.

'This one's dead, Sheriff!' one called across to him.

'Anybody know him?' he called back.

'Nope, he ain't bin in Hudson afore.' This came emphatically from Flory Brock, a scarred veteran of the Mexican wars, who knew every man, woman and horse in the county.

Citizens clustered around Emerson's tall figure as he stood punching fresh shells into his Colt, and from the babble of voices rising about him now he was getting a vividly clear picture of what had taken place.

The drama had begun when four men had ridden in singly and quietly to tether their mounts at the hitchrail by Hogan's Store adjacent to the bank.

One had remained with the mounts while the others had entered the building quietly. In the blink of an eye the trio had tugged bandannas up over their faces and bailed up customers and staff from behind naked six-guns.

Head teller Tolliver had snatched up a sawed-off but was pistol-whipped off his feet. Dobbs had frozen helplessly with a revolver rammed into his back before the bandits had set about scooping up several thousand dollars' worth of old and new bank notes.

Bellowing warnings to stay put, the bandits were then backing for the doors when the Widow Evers collapsed from sheer terror. This had caused a momentary distraction but it was long enough for Dobbs and a recovered Tolliver to go for their guns.

Dobbs instantly stopped a slug in the back but somehow managed to make it to the steps before collapsing. The outlaw leader, the man upon the big red horse, made to drill Dobbs where he'd fallen when Tolliver had rushed at him, only to be belted unconscious by a sweeping blow from a six-shooter barrel. The outlaw was about to pump a slug into the fallen figure when their leader bawled an order and the survivors instantly took flight in a wild thunder of hoofbeats.

'What are we gonna do, Jack?' a cowboy yelled excitedly.

'Go get 'em, of course,' Emerson replied grimly.

He swung to confront the mob assembling in the street. 'I'm calling for volunteers to form up a posse. Go get yourselves some grub, shells and weather gear then meet me back here in no longer than five minutes. No bunch of scum can hold up this town and get away with it!'

Without exception every able-bodied man broke away to head pell-mell for the livery stables, and a motley bunch they were – storekeepers, cowhands and white-handed clerks. They didn't look much as they came rushing back leading horses several minutes later. But Emerson knew what they were made of and felt proud of their readiness to go after a dangerous a bunch of hellers without regard for the risk involved.

'Garcia,' he said to the Mexican boy at his side, 'go saddle my bay and get my Winchester from the rack.' He tossed the kid a key. 'And pack my saddle-bags with tinned beans, beef and a pound of Arbuckle's coffee.'

'*Sí*, Señor Emerson,' the kid said excitedly, and was gone in a blur of sun-browned legs.

By now Dobbs had been toted inside the bank. Emerson strode across to the hitchrail where a bunch had clustered around the dead outlaw who lay sprawled on his back, face the colour of old pipe clay.

The mob parted and the peace officer stared down at the man he had shot.

He looked around thirty with the punched-in face of a brawler, a rat-trap mouth. Jack went through the dead outlaw's pockets. He found virtually nothing but the stub of a ticket with the printing almost obliterated, but with some difficulty finally deciphered the name, Zebulon.

'Sheriff!'

Deputy Fulton came pushing through the crowd nursing a bloodstained right arm.

'What happened, Sam? You're hurt!'

'Just nicked, Sheriff,' Fulton replied, his pallor suggesting he lied. 'I run out at the first shot and got sat on my rear end by a slug from this no-account lying here. I musta passed out,' he added in disgust.

Jack clapped his shoulder. 'You go get seen to, pronto. I'm taking a posse out after them. You'll be in charge here till I get back.'

'Right, Sheriff. Say, any notion who they were?'

Again Emerson frowned at the grubby stub in his fingers. 'Maybe . . . not sure. That pilgrim had this on him. It's from Zebulon.'

Fulton stared blankly a moment before his eyes snapped wide. 'Zebulon! Damnit, that's the place the Rangers wired us about . . . the place that was shot up by the Ketchell gang!'

Ketchell!

The name seemed to hit every man hard – and every eye suddenly focused upon the tall figure of Jack Emerson. For the outlaw Ketchell's reign of terror had earned him wide notoriety across southwest Texas in recent times, and now it seemed that hellion had struck right here in Hudson – hometown of his sister and his brother-in-law – Sheriff Jack Emerson!

The lawman's pale face was stripped of all expression as he nodded and turned to Fulton.

'It might well have been Blain Ketchell,' he conceded grimly. 'Matter of fact I'd got word recent he could be pushing south. I recall the Rangers reporting he was riding a big red gelding when last seen ... and one of those masked hellers was forking a mount just like that—'

He broke off on realizing most of the men were already saddled and ready for the trail. Quickly he issued final instructions to the deputy, then swung up. The bay horse danced in the dust and he patted the silken neck.

'Send a wire to Captain Will Calice of the Seventh Company, Texas Rangers, in Zebulon,' he ordered. 'Give him a full report and say we suspect the Ketchell bunch. If he's not there, make certain they send the message on to him. That's it!'

He flipped Garcia a dollar, checked out his saddle-bags then signalled to the eager riders.

They fell in behind him as he led the way down Buffalo Street at the trot before kicking the horse into a lope. Within minutes they were gone from sight, swallowed up in the heat and dust of the west Texas plains.

CHAPTER 2

HEADIN' WEST

Leaving the town marker far behind in his dust the sheriff settled his mount down to a steady mile-eating lope with grim-faced possemen following hard behind.

The bank robbers had taken the main trail south from Hudson, their tracks were clear in the thick dust which made sign-reading unnecessary and so enabled Emerson to set a brisk pace.

The trail stretched almost dead straight ahead for several miles at this stage of the pursuit, a brown and narrow strip separating fenced rangelands. Soon the land grew increasingly undulating with timber and shrub growing more thickly. Yet still the bandits had stuck to the main trail, causing the lawman to puzzle as to just what destination his quarry had in mind.

He decided that the very fact that the bunch wasn't making for the high brush country indicated they intended trying simply to outrun any pursuit. Then again, it could just as easily mean the outlaws were figuring nobody would have the guts to follow them even this far.

He calculated the time elapsing since the recent robbery over in Zebulon until this latest incident. It was a fair distance from Zebulon to Hudson, which suggested that the killers' mounts by now would have to be heavy-legged from the many miles they'd covered.

He frowned.

Yet if that were the case, he wondered, why in hell had they hit the bank that way then taken off along the main trail without making any attempt to blot their sign?

Could this simply be a gesture of contempt?

That thought touched off a strong suspicion that Blain Ketchell might indeed have been that tall, masked leader of the bunch. For Ketchell the outlaw had been both audacious and successful over recent months, and maybe he'd reckoned a small town like Hudson should prove a walkover

. . . while showing no regard for the fact that his own sister was the sheriff's wife there!

The party clattered across the stony dry bed at Pitanda Creek then allowed the horses to drop back to a shuffling walk-trot to ascend the steep shale shelf beyond, which led them on upwards to the harsh and hostile plateau country further on. And dimly visible upon the far south-western horizon from their elevated position now was the distant line of gaunt stone pinnacles reaching into the skies . . . the beginning of the Badlands. . . .

The heat was already taking its toll: kerchiefs mopping damp faces . . . shirts clinging stickily to sweating backs . . . animals lathered and blowing hard as that brassy sun hammered down.

And still the chase went on.

The sign grew less distinct where it threaded over miles of rock and shale yet was still clear enough to Emerson's keen eye to enable him to maintain a steady pace.

Only occasionally did he allow himself to dwell on the bitter irony of a lawman setting out to catch or maybe even kill his own wife's brother. This surely was a case of the devil rolling destiny's dice! Yet if there was a brighter side it was the harsh reality that his Carmel and her outlaw brother Blain had been estranged, one from the other, ever since childhood. He'd always sensed that the man's outlawry had obliterated any feelings his sister may have once held for him.

The trail led around a mighty, red-rock butte looming two hundred feet above the baking landscape.

They welcomed the brief shade which protected them from the brutal blast of the sun, but when they emerged it seemed to have grown even hotter in the wake of their momentary respite.

Then every rider's thoughts were abruptly diverted from heat and sweat as Emerson suddenly stood in his stirrups and let out a yell.

'Look!' He gestured far ahead to where a column of butter-coloured dust was now visible climbing sluggishly into the still afternoon sky and showing starkly against the background of the dark stone of the Sangre de Cristo peaks.

'That's them, sure enough!' Seth Brey declared breathlessly. 'Less riders than started out, but enough of them, and still ridin' hard. It's got to be them! Could be we'll get to run the bastards down now!'

They halted eagerly around Emerson to study the distant cloud when he called a canteen break. Spirits were high now and someone bragged, 'We'll show all Texas that no bunch of low killers can rob the honest folk of Hudson and get away with it! Right, Sheriff?'

But even if Jack Emerson shared their general confidence at this sighting he was far from claiming victory just yet. He had a hunch this really was their quarry far ahead – yet experience and instinct warned that a chase like this was likely still a long way from over.

The unfamiliar terrain stretching into infinity appeared hostile and alien to the eye. He also knew that if a man travelled far enough south-west out there he would eventually come to the deserts and badlands of the southlands that were so vast and hostile that little was known about them other than that any Texan who truly valued his life simply never ventured there.

Yet they wouldn't be diverted today.

This chase would end when they ran their quarry down and not before, he vowed. Yet grimly determined though he might be, he still hoped they would run the bunch down before they got to the real deserts, for out there in that burning back of beyond known as the Texas Badlands, effective manhunting would likely prove impossible or even suicidal.

He was about to use his heels when something else different about the sign caught his eye. He reined in and jumped down, flipped his reins to a rider then walked slowly on ahead to study the clear hoof marks showing in the dust and shale at this point.

After some time he halted and glanced back to summon Walt Holly, veteran plainsman and desert hunter.

'How many horses you figure in this bunch now, Walt?'

'Looks like just three or four animals, Sheriff,' came the drawled reply. 'Although I gotta admit it's hard to be sure.'

'What are we delayin' for, Jack?' Seth Brey demanded impatiently. 'Them there tracks are plain as paint even to an old squinter like myself. Every minute we waste here lets them murdering skunks stretch their lead.'

Jack ignored the protest. 'Step down and take a closer look at these tracks, Walt.'

Walt Holly did as ordered, a man as lean and hungry looking as an old coyote, yet still as keen of eye as a peregrine falcon. He studied the sign for a time before he stiffened and glanced back sharply.

'I'll be sheep-dipped!' he exclaimed, scratching the back of his head. 'There's five of 'em now. Where'd that fifth varmint come from? And why would anybody hitch up with a bunch of owlhoots on the dodge with an angry posse snortin' down their necks?'

'Don't ask me,' Jack grunted. 'But I guess we can be pretty sure that's what's happened here.'

'No doubt about it, boy, for sign don't lie. But it don't change nothin', does it? Four, five or however many, we're still gonna nail 'em. Right?'

Other voices sounded in support yet Emerson remained quiet and thoughtful. This additional set of tracks was a puzzle that he wanted to try to figure out – if only he had that sort of time.

Returning to the group he filled leather then swung around and turned back to head towards the red butte!

Seth Brey came spurring after him.

'What the hell you doin'?'

'Just my job,' he replied tersely. 'So, no more jaw. If you don't like the way I'm running this hunt, then get on back to town.'

The man flushed angrily but didn't retort as Emerson turned and beckoned Holly across. The two moved on ahead together to scout the terrain surrounding the towering butte.

It wasn't long before Emerson halted and indicated footmarks on the ground. 'There,' he said. 'This extra man was waiting for them here. He had to know they were coming, is my best guess.'

Holly nodded and lighted up, sucking smoke deep into his lungs. The man appeared to grow more puzzled as he studied the sign more closely.

He turned sharply to gaze over the brooding landscape far to the south-west. He didn't know this country, scarce anyone did. Badlands, they were called, and that was all any westerner needed to know to avoid them. Nothing out there but dust and heat and likely quick death – or leastwise so most Texans believed.

'Well, what the hell difference does it make?' a rider finally grouched. 'Four, five, a dozen – we got rope enough aplenty to hang 'em all.'

Others voiced their support, while Emerson began backtracking the sign left by that fifth rider. This eventually led him to one single clear boot-heel print in a patch of firm ground where most everything else was loose and sandy.

It was no everyday print he realized as he dismounted and hunkered down. No workman or cowboy had left this mark, but someone who sported a flashy high boot-heel, which seemed at the same moment both unusual yet somehow familiar. . . .

He glanced up sharply to see Holly scratching his head. 'This feller must be some heck of a flash dude to wear show-off boots like that away out here in the boondocks I reckon, eh, Sheriff?'

'Yeah . . . *some* dude all right. . . .'

Emerson began to circle afoot. He moved slowly and deliberately, keen eye missing no detail. Once he halted to retrieve a half-smoked cheroot butt. When he glanced back over his shoulder he saw Holly looking bored as he gazed off into the hazy distance.

Soon he'd seen enough. He slipped the butt into his shirt pocket and returned to his horse to swing up in silence and led them back to join the others.

'Well, we getting on after them now, Sheriff?' Brey wanted to know. 'If we give them much more slack we'll have a real hard time running them down before dark.'

The others grouped around to wait for a reply. Emerson took his time, and when he finally spoke it came as a shock.

'We're returning to Hudson,' he announced quietly.

Everybody gaped. 'Quit now?' Seth Brey gasped. 'In nation's name – why, man?'

'Simple,' Emerson replied. 'We couldn't run them down before dark, which means we'd be camping out overnight which would give them a good ten hours of darkness to make it to wherever it is they're heading; likely the badlands around Silver, is my guess. That means we couldn't run them to ground in that hell country tomorrow even if we rode all night.'

'Hell, man, you want a whole posse to quit on a bunch of killers when they're likely dropping in their tracks and just waiting to be picked up. I don't believe it.'

'He's right, Jack—' Otter Brawling began, but Emerson cut him off.

'I'm bossing this chase,' he said with authority. 'That means I'm responsible for everybody here. The way I read it – the gang is too far ahead now, and that extra gun tips the odds against us. So now I mean to hand the job of running them down over to the Rangers.'

It was some time before Seth Brey broke the silence. 'So, why'd you bring us all this way if you didn't plan to see it through, Sheriff?'

'Yeah,' Brawling chimed in. 'Hell, if I didn't know you better, Emerson, I might suspect you were packin' it up on account of Ketchell bein' your wife's brother.'

Jack dragged deeply on his cigarette. He appeared unfazed by the accusation – and was. He'd never made any apology for his wife being a Ketchell. But this was not a debate he would resurrect here. And the star on his vest said he still called the shots.

He faced them squarely. 'We're heading back to town. Any man who wants to keep on after Ketchell is free to do so . . . I'll see he gets a proper funeral.'

With that he filled leather and heeled away around the butte base.

Reaching the trail an hour later he swung east for Hudson. Emerging from lengthening shadows he glanced back to see that all save Seth and Otter were trailing. That pair appeared to be still wrangling. He had several uneasy moments before they too finally kicked on after on him, yet the pair were plainly still angry and made no attempt to bridge that gap and stayed far back all the long way to Hudson.

The ride back to town seemed to take forever. The high spirits and thirst for reprisal that had fired their outward journey was totally gone and it was plain that the town couldn't appear quickly enough now.

Jack continued to ride well ahead and alone, conscious of accusing eyes boring his back but paying no heed.

It was late afternoon when they reached their

destination with deep shadows lying across the streets and the first tinkling music drifting from the saloons. Citizens emerged to watch them ride by, hopeful looks fading fast when they saw no sign of prisoners or bodies draped over bloodied saddles.

One by one the possemen peeled off while Emerson continued on to the jailhouse.

Deputy Fulton emerged with one arm in a sling to receive a terse account of the manhunt, which ended when Seth Brey rode into sight. Emerson called to the man and the three entered the law office where Fulton already had one lantern lighted. For a moment Jack savoured the welcome familiarity of the place, then shook his head wearily, placed his rifle back in the rack and squarely faced men who'd never seen him more serious.

Wordlessly he unpinned his star and dropped it upon the desk.

'That's it. I'm quitting!'

Brey and Fulton gaped uncomprehendingly. Then both began speaking at once. He let them protest for a brief spell then held up a hand for silence.

'All your jaw isn't going to change anything,' he stated flatly. 'I've made a decision and it's final.

Sam, you can take over here; you know as much about the job as I do. Both of you are good men. I'm sorry, but this is just the way it has to be.'

Both were still protesting vigorously when he walked outside, swung astride his horse and headed for home.

Carmel appeared almost immediately. She hurried towards him as he dismounted but hesitated uncertainly upon seeing his face so tight and pale.

'Honey,' she cried, taking his arm. 'What's wrong? Are you all right? Where's your star?'

Calmly and quietly he told her of his discovery and subsequent decision to return to the town.

He told her directly that the set of tracks he'd examined in the wilds revealed that one of the outlaws was her kid brother, Danny.

It was one of the hardest things he'd ever been called upon to do. Yet she was a lawman's wife and proved it by remaining calm, despite the obvious shock.

'Are . . . are you sure there's no doubt, honey?' she asked hopefully as they entered the house. 'Perhaps—'

'His footprints are out there along with the tracks of his horse, Carmel.' He shook his head. 'It was him.'

It grew quiet in the room, a silence that appeared to stretch on forever. Having an outlaw as a brother had been a cross for Carmel Emerson to bear for a long time. But the realization that Danny had joined the bank robbers was like a dagger-thrust to the heart.

It seemed a long time before she found her voice again.

'And . . . and that's the reason you're resigning, Jack? Surely—'

'There's only one way to do this thing,' he said, moving about the room, grim-faced and purposeful. 'He's got to be brought in . . . but that could take weeks, maybe months. This town can't function without a sheriff that long and I can't expect it to.'

He shrugged then rested both hands gently on her shoulders.

'But you understand the real reason I have to do it this way, don't you? Danny is my kin by marriage and it just wouldn't be right – a sheriff hunting his own brother-in-law. All that gossip if I failed, the suspicions. No, I've got to—'

'But, Jack, even if you feel you have to resign, surely that doesn't mean you have any obligation to risk your life as you would be doing if you went into that hideous desert. Nobody would expect—'

'Honey, this isn't my fault, and it sure as hell is not yours. But the law demands that because of my experience and the fact that I know your brother well means that it's my obligation to bring him in.' He paused for a moment, then honesty forced him to add, 'Either dead or alive. . . .'

When Carmel made no response he glanced at her. She was deathly pale, her eyes appearing enormous and stricken. He gripped her hands, knowing what she had to be going through.

But she turned away slowly and stood by the window, gazing out.

'There's no other way?' she asked quietly, knowing what the answer had to be.

He shook his head. 'The way I see it all now, Blain must have learned of the money they were holding at the bank and decided to help himself. Somehow he contacted Danny and conned him into joining him – that foolish, foolish boy!'

He had a brief image in his mind of Danny's dark eyes dancing excitedly as the dashing Blain recounted stories of adventure and danger to be had on the owlhoot . . . most likely without once even hinting at the reality that danger and sudden death dogged any outlaw's every waking moment. . . .

He went on deliberately. 'Guess he figured

Danny would be a good man to add to his bunch with that lightning draw of his.'

She stood facing him now.

'Jack, you say that Danny likely only joined up with them after the robbery. Would that mean he's not really guilty of any crime?'

'Not yet, leastways.'

'Then you simply *must* find him, darling,' she said with sudden strength and certainty. 'I know that's why you felt you must hand in your badge, and I love you for it.' She came into his arms, the trembling shaking her whole body now. 'Find him, Jack . . . please find him before it is too late, before he is either shot or hanged – or before Blain turns him into a monster like himself.'

'I will,' he promised. 'I know what he means to you, and he means just as much to me too.'

For a long moment they clung together, each acutely aware of what lay ahead – the separation for perhaps days or weeks, or even longer. For Texas was vast, although few knew it better than Jack Emerson. Finally and with reluctance, he held her at arms' length.

'I've got to go.'

Without a word she led him inside the house where she prepared his saddle-bags, packing in salt, flour, salt pork and coffee. She buckled up his war bag then checked out his rifle and six-gun, as only a lawman's wife could. Everything was in readinesss within the half-hour and while he went outside to roll his warbags and lash them to the saddle, she prepared coffee.

They drank together almost in silence, the brooding uncertainty of the future weighing down heavily upon both. Then he kissed her goodbye on the porch and walked off down the pathway to the gate.

'Take care,' she called softly.

'Surely,' he murmured, climbing into the saddle. '*Adios.*'

She watched as he rode from sight into the night and the tears she had held back with such difficulty sprang to her eyes. She remained there alone on the porch a long time, a small, slim figure watching the great, golden moon begin its reign . . . that same moon which would also be lighting the path of the wild, dark-haired brother she loved . . . out there . . . somewhere. . . .

'Danny!' she whispered brokenly. 'Oh, Danny boy. . . .'

CHAPTER 3

GUNSMOKE SUNDOWN

Blain Ketchell wiped the lenses of his binoculars with a yellow kerchief and again trained them upon the base of the gaunt red butte which reared up abruptly from the prairie floor several miles to the north.

The posse had been milling around for some time away back there and he was still puzzled as to what they were doing. Not that he was complaining. Each additional minute those rubes wasted added to the recovery time he was able to give the horses, which they really needed by this time.

'They still out there, Blain?'

The man who spoke was Irby Tebbs, a thin and bitter-faced man with a voice right off the head of a banjo. He was lounging in the shade of a cottonwood with Cull Winster, a bulky redhead, who was strapping up a bullet crease in a hairy calf muscle.

'Yeah,' grunted Ketchell. 'Come take a look, Danny.'

The slim youth who had been standing by the tethered mounts moved across to his brother's side. His walk was lithe and quick as were all his movements. He was of medium height with a handsome, sun-browned face. He sported a flashy red shirt and his feet were encased in high-heeled and flashy cowboy boots. Low on his right hip he wore a pearl-handled Colt .45, still shining with newness.

He took the proffered glasses and studied the far-off group intently.

'They're quitting!' he finally exclaimed.

'What?' Ketchell said. 'Here, gimme them glasses, kid.'

A broad grin split the outlaw's features when he put the instrument to his eyes. For the distant horsemen were indeed turning back along the old Hudson trail ... or all but two, that was, as he quickly realized. As the column moved off he focused upon the pair remaining but couldn't figure what was holding them. But after a time they also rode off, all but disappearing in the dust raised by those ahead.

He turned with a triumphant grin to the youth, then signalled to the other pair by the tree. 'They've cut and run, boys. All those big brave towners have high-tailed it back to Hudson and their mammies. We're free as jay birds.'

'More damn luck than anything iffen you ask me,' muttered gloomy Winster, still busy with his leg.

'Give me another look with them there glasses, Blain,' Danny insisted.

The youth focused upon the distant movement until the figures became mere dots upon the trail. There could be no doubt the party was making back for Hudson. As he lowered the glasses with a grin, his brother was watching him closely.

'Glad he's quit, eh, kid?'

'Huh? Oh, yeah . . . guess so.'

'Uh-huh. Could've been kinda messy if they'd run us down.'

Danny glanced swiftly at his brother. Had he detected something in the brother's tone, a note almost of disappointment, maybe?

'You think I might be scared of facing Jack, Blain?' he challenged. 'Hell no, that's not it. I knew when I joined up with you that I'd likely see my share of gunplay. No sir, it sure wasn't that,' he insisted, yet glanced quickly away as if fearing the other might suspect the real reason for his relief.

'Let me guess,' Ketchell said shrewdly. 'You wasn't keen to trade lead maybe with your old hero pal, Emerson? That's it, right?'

Danny just shrugged, well aware that his brother had hit home. In the exciting two days since his long-missing outlaw brother had ridden into Hudson and fired up his imagination with tales of his reckless, free-wheeling life outside the law, Danny's one concern had been Jack Emerson. He knew he wasn't scared of the man, for the reality was simply that he knew he was much swifter than just about anybody with the clean and draw. But he respected the lawman and doubted very much that he would ever be able to draw on him were they ever to come face to face.

Blain clapped him on the back, and laughed.

'No shame in bein' loyal to an old pal, kid. But we got the dinero and we got away without a scratch, so my invitin' you along has played out just fine.' He lowered his voice and nodded at the other two men, winked. 'Anyway, a man like me needs a side-kick he can *trust*.'

Danny flushed with pleasure. He needed reassurance right now because he was already vaguely fearing he'd succumbed too quickly to his brother's inducements to join the bunch. Sure, it had been as exciting as hell – the action back there. He loved excitement and it was great riding with Blain. Even so, he often felt low and only hoped it didn't show.

'Well, pards,' Blain declared, circling the small fire with hands jammed in hip pockets, 'we got us the dinero and got off without more'n a scratch or two just like I said we would. Correct?'

'Old Murt Bronson never got off,' Cull replied sullenly, glancing up from ugly yellow-flecked eyes. 'Old Murt was a good pard of mine. Sure gonna miss him around, that's for certain.'

'Nobody lives forever,' Blain said airily. 'What happened to him was just the luck of the draw. We all run the same risk in this man's outfit.'

'Not all,' growled Winster, shifting his gaze to new recruit Danny. 'Some of us don't get to take no risk at all.'

There was sudden tension in the air; you could feel it.

The Ketchell gang had been holed up outside Hudson after eventually eluding a Texas Ranger posse which had clung to their trail over several days.

They'd looked forward to a lay-off but leader

Blain had other plans. Some time back he'd checked out the Hudson Bank and decided it was ripe for the picking. The job had gone well but the others were sore when Ketchell showed up afterwards with his kid brother in tow, then introduced him as a new gang member.

A green kid could mean trouble, they believed. Their resentment had deepened when Blain forbade Danny to play any active part in the hold-up in town, but instead gave him the safe chore of watching out for the sheriff.

'Sometimes you talk too much, Cull,' Ketchell said quietly.

He stood in the flooding sunlight, tall and lean with thumbs hooked in shell belt and strong teeth showing whitely in a deeply tanned face. Despite that smile, Winster sensed menace in his words and grumblingly focused his attention upon his bullet-grazed leg again.

Blain swung back to Danny with a chuckle. 'Old Cull's always tetchy when he's shot up. So . . . how do you like the life so far, kid? Easy dough, huh?'

'Not for Bronson, it wasn't,' Danny stated, thinking of the dead man and how he'd died.

Blain's smile vanished as he clapped a hand to Danny's shoulder.

'Lesson number one,' he counselled, 'never fret

over the fallen. That can bring a man undone. Just think, Old Murt had a fair bite of the cherry and when he died he went quick and easy. . . .'

He abruptly dropped his hand and turned sober.

'That was your brother-in-law that bored Old Murt . . . got real gun savvy, that feller. It was sure lucky you was able to tell us how Emerson always got home for chow right on time since he got wedded, on account that made it real easy for us to nail the bank. I gotta say now I wouldn't fancy that one breathing down my neck while I was busy pullin' a job.'

Danny remained silent. He suddenly had the feeling too much had happened too fast since he'd joined the bunch for the raid on the Hudson Bank. Seemed he could still hear the gunfire as the gang had thundered out of town. . . .

Ketchell seemed unaware of his kid brother's silence as he drew a thin cigarillo from a breast pocket and set it between his teeth then set a match to it. Exhaling, he stared off absently at the horses drowsing in the sweaty shade and twitching wearily at the flies.

'It don't figure,' he declared at length.

'What don't?' twanged lanky Irby Tebbs, coming to his feet and stretching.

'That there posse turnin' back the way it did . . .

somehow that just don't add up. . . .'

'Hell, you ain't complainin', are you?' Winster grumbled. 'We been choused and hounded so much lately I was beginnin' to feel like a jackrabbit.'

'I ain't complaining,' Ketchell said. 'But I don't fancy things happening that I don't rightly understand.' He dragged on his stogie and glanced at Danny. 'You got any notion why they quit on us the way they just done, kid?'

'No. Jack's never let anyone just get away on him before.'

'Yeah, well mebbe that's on account he never had Blain Ketchell to deal with before,' the outlaw boasted. He headed for the horses. 'Let's ride.'

'What for?' Winster demanded peevishly, indicating his heavily strapped lower limb. 'There ain't nobody pressin' us right now and this is givin' me gyp.'

Ketchell untethered his mount and swung astride. Cigar jutting from his teeth he drew up by the cottonwood and stared down at the wounded badman, dark eyes glittering.

'Mount up or stay and rot, Winster, I don't give a damn!' He slapped fat saddle-bags. 'But this here dinero travels with me.'

Resentment flared in Winster's yellow eyes, yet

he got to his feet without delay and headed for the remuda. Likewise, Irby Tebbs lost no time filling leather and soon, in single file with Blain leading and Danny bringing up the rear, the bunch headed on out.

Riding into the afternoon they drove ever deeper into the tumbling, tawny harshness of the southwest Texas plains, leaving behind the cottonwoods and elm and encountering the first odd stands of giant cactus as they travelled on, sure signs the deserts and real badlands were drawing ever closer.

Ketchell kept his mount to a steady gait, hat tilted forwards against the glare as his eyes restlessly probed the way ahead. Once he halted to climb a hill to survey the country on all sides with field glasses. When no distant dust cloud indicated pursuit he resumed his position in the lead with an air of satisfaction and headed on.

From time to time he would reach back and feel the solid weight of the satchels containing what had formerly been the cash currency of the Hudson Bank. He quit grinning whenever he recalled that gruelling flight from Zebulon with Calice's Rangers breathing down his neck prior to that event.

So he deliberately allowed his mind to focus upon the Ranger captain.

He'd only sighted him once from hiding in an Austin alley, yet carried a clear impression in his mind. It wasn't a pleasant recollection, for that manhunter was outsized, incorruptible and ugly as sin.

He'd first picked up on rumours that a small company of Texas Rangers was out hunting him some three months earlier, but had not believed it prior to that close shave back at Zebulon.

That was how the law had captured Sam Bass's outfit, he reflected – setting a squad of Rangers on his trail with orders not to come back until they'd bagged their man.

He experienced a moment's unease at the recollection, yet his overpowering self-assurance quickly returned. For Bass had finally come to grief trying nobly to save the neck of one of his henchmen following a big robbery and lawmen on the chase.

His lip curled in a sneer. No chance of his going down that way. No room for sentiment in the outlaw trade – or loyalty either for that matter. Not in his book. You pulled your job, the leader got the lion's share and anyone who didn't like it could either quit or face fast Blain.

The trail they now followed entered a wide, shallow arroyo studded with brave patches of green mescal. Dust rose in lethargic puffs at the horses' every step and wisped sluggishly away.

There were times on a remote trail like this that a man might imagine he could smell the wild scent of the Staked Plains, a country vast, mysterious and hostile enough to raise even Ketchell's neck hair at times. Most called them the Staked Plains but others knew it as the Land of the Comancheros.

The killer shivered involuntarily. He was as tough and gutsy as they came yet whispers or bloody tales from Comanchero country never left him unmoved for some reason.

Emerging from an echoing arroyo several hours later, their way led across the Butterfield stage route from Georgeville to far distant Hudson, the plains now stretching away mournfully empty on all sides.

They clattered across the stage road and travelled on.

Cull Winster hipped around in his saddle to squint enviously at the far distant trail running away towards Silver, as he clutched at his throbbing leg.

There was a sawbones' attention and rye whiskey to be had in that man's town – if he was let take that route. A big *if*. He stared sullenly at Ketchell's sweaty back now. No point in griping to him any longer. A man could come down with gangrene for all Ketchell cared. One day . . . someday . . . Ketchell could go too far and Winster might slip a six-shooter silently from a well-greased holster and give him six in the back. Until then? Well, maybe gangrene wasn't really as bad as some claimed. . . .

Feeling the sudden need for company the outlaw moved his mount forward to range abreast of Irby Tebbs. Tebbs, slumped low in his Texas-Spanish saddle, looked even more forbidding than usual with white alkaline dust coating his ugly face and sweat running from thick greasy hair in tiny rivulets.

A loner whom nobody knew much about, Tebbs was a fast man with a Colt .45. You needed to be to hold your place in this outfit. The man kept to himself and never talked much, and this usually discouraged Winster. He was put off afresh now when the other turned bleak eyes to stare at him in silence – the way a hungry buzzard might. But before Winster could react the leader's harsh voice sounded up ahead; 'Break off for a spell!'

The party swung down in the shade of a giant cottonwood. It was almost cool and both Winster and Tebbs set about unsaddling quickly in order to take full advantage of however much leisure time Ketchell might dole out.

All then relaxed to ease weary bones with Danny

perching on a fallen tree and the others favouring the soft earth where they rested to watch Ketchell rake the alien countryside with his hattered field glasses.

Some time later he replaced the binoculars in their case, spat cotton, took a sparing sip from his canteen then lighted up a long thin stogie. 'Time we split up,' he announced abruptly.

Both Winston and Tebbs sat up and stared at him. This was the first they'd heard of any split-up. Ketchell returned their looks with a smirk.

'No surprises,' he declared. 'You all know I never keep any bunch together long. That ain't my way. Besides, that goddamn Calice likely knows all about the stick-up by now. You can bet your last pair of boots he'll be huffin' and pantin' on our tracks soon as he can find them. We'll all move faster and safer when we're broken up. OK?'

The two hardcases didn't like it. The term safety in numbers had real meaning when one of those numbers happened to be Ketchell.

Tebbs considered what had been said briefly then turned to his henchman.

'Reckon he's right?'

'Could be . . . just could be,' Winster replied. He'd been taken by surprise by the sudden decision yet realized that with his cut of the hold-up he could now head off into Silver and spell up – maybe even get his leg tended to. Minutes before he'd been all set to tackle Ketchell about that but now realized he could be on his way without any wrangling.

He rose and stretched. 'Powerful good notion, Blain. Guess I ain't too keen on us splittin' up but like you say, we got a better chance of slippin' the law thataways.'

Ketchell stared hard at the bulky badman.

'I'd wager my cut of the take that I can guess where you're going to make for first thing, Winster,' he growled.

Winster looked blank for a moment. 'Huh?' he grunted. 'How you figure?'

'Because I read you like big print, of course.' Ketchell got to his feet to glance across at Danny. 'You know what he means to do, kid? He's going to hot-lick it straight to Silver and then tie into the liquor, the gals and the hoop-de-doo.' He swung sharply on Winster, whose jaw now hung foolishly open. 'That's right, ain't it, Cull?'

'Yeah ... well, guess it is,' Winster admitted, bridling at Ketchell's sarcasm. He realized he would be glad to see the last of this half-smart hardcase.

Ketchell grinned through his cigar smoke and

strolled lazily across to his horse and began to unstrap the money-sacks.

'You ain't bright,' he said, with his back to them yet loud enough for all to hear. 'Not bright at all. I'll tell you why.' He turned his head. 'You recall how we set down a false trail for the Rangers to sniff on after we headed to Hudson?'

'Yeah, but—' Winster began, but got no further before he was cut off.

'Sure you do,' Ketchell said loudly, returning with the sacks. 'But what you don't recall is that the false lead headed straight for Silver. I figure that if Calice ain't there now, he's already been and gone and likely left some posters with our mugs on them at the law office. That one don't ever overlook too much.'

Winster sensed this reasoning could well be accurate, and flushed with embarrassment at his own stupidity.

Caution warned him to keep shut but his anger was the stronger. 'So, what is it like to know every goddamn thing – all the goddamn time?' he said loudly.

The atmosphere chilled at that, bringing both Danny and Tebbs to their feet. Ketchell deliberately lowered the sacks to the ground, his smile still in place but the eyes now cold as sleet.

Winster, realizing he had gone too far, was still sore enough to be reckless. He stood wide-legged glaring at Ketchell and breathing noisily through his mouth.

'Steady on now,' came Irby Tebbs's quiet warning as he stepped between the pair. 'Cull, you just simmer down, boy. What Blain said was mostly likely right, y'know.'

'Oh, yeah?' Winster snapped heatedly. 'He's always goddamn right – and I can tell you I've had a bellyfull of that, and of him too if you want to know the truth.'

'Free country.' Ketchell's tone was calm and cold. 'So what do you plan to do about all that . . . pardner?' he added, while dropping right hand close to gun butt.

This time Tebbs swung to face him squarely and his tough little gunslinger's face was pale and taut. 'Just leave him be, Blain. Seems like you both been out under the sun too long. It's way too late in the game to start scrappin' over nothin'. What say we just divvy up the take and split?' A pause. 'OK?'

Ketchell's testiness seemed to vanish at that. He grinned broadly. 'Sure, it's fine. Hell, what are we scrappin' for anyways? C'mon, let's split her up.'

Winster's temper cooled before Ketchell's easy manner and the three promptly hunkered down to count the fat wads of notes they took from the sacks.

Danny finger-combed his thick hair and sat on a deadfall some distance away, looking on. His expression was blank but underneath he was tense. As well as a frighteningly fast right hand, he had a sixth sense for trouble. This was nagging at him right now, and it was something it never paid to ignore.

Eventually, Ketchell rose with a smile and nodded to the youth. 'Twelve thousand bucks, kid. Not too dusty for five minutes work, huh?'

'Not bad . . . no sir!'

'Sure 'nuff.' Ketchell chuckled and began to count silently on his fingers as though grappling with weighty mathematical calculations.

Tebbs rose and came as close as anyone had ever seen to smiling. 'Heck, no need to go to all that trouble to figure the cuts, Ketch. Three into twelve comes to four thousand apiece.'

Ketchell looked up in seeming surprise. 'Three into twelve thousand, you say? Four, Irby, *four*!'

Tebb's smile vanished as if it had never existed.

'What do you mean – *four*? Bronson's dead!'

'Oh, I ain't talkin' about old Murt.' He paused to count on his fingers. 'You, Cull, me and Danny – four.'

A sudden silence came down over the group like a cloud. Tebbs, Winster and Danny all stared at Ketchell whose expression remained bland, if watchful. After recovering some, Tebbs glared across at Winster and Danny, then cut angry eyes back to Ketchell.

'You better be goddamned jokin', Ketchell. Four of us pulled that job while the kid was safe and sound way out on the trail. We ran the risks and threw the lead. So the take gets split three ways – *even?!*'

'That's fair, Blain, I didn't earn any cut.' Danny was as puzzled as any at his brother's proposal, just as he'd been confused earlier when it seemed Blain was trying to goad Winster into a fight.

'I make the decisions here, kid,' Ketchell drawled. 'I say it's a four-way split, so that's how it stands. *Compre?*'

Tebbs went back a pace, seeming to crouch slightly with right hand close to gun handle. Winster, both perplexed and angered, moved closer to him. Ketchell stood lazily off to one side with a faint smile touching his lips as he stole a quick glance at Danny.

Danny, though new to the owlhoot, was savvy enough to scent trouble in the suddenly highly charged air. He didn't understand what was happening, only knew Blain was in some kind of danger. He took a long step forward to confront the threatening pair.

Tebbs cast a swift glance at him then returned to Blain.

'You got one chance, Ketchell. Divvy up three ways and we'll just ride out. Otherwise you're buzzard meat on account we both know I could outdraw you on the fastest day you ever lived.'

'Maybe, Irby . . . just maybe.' Ketchell conceded. 'But what you ain't, is as fast as the kid.'

Tebbs was incredulous.

'You – you're leanin' on *him?*'

'Uh-huh.' Ketchell appeared calm and untroubled. 'You recall what I said about maybe needin' you one day, Danny boy?'

Suddenly the explosive Tebbs had heard enough. With a snarling curse he went low with right hand whipping for the gun riding his hip.

In a single moment, four hands grabbed for guns. But it was Danny's piece that roared and belched fierce gun flame first. The bullet caught Irby Tebbs high in the temple and almost ripped off the top of his skull as he was hurled backwards with the unfired .45 tumbling from his dead hand.

Winster's Colt was out but Danny's next bullet thudded into his body, followed by another and yet another, the three shots sounding almost like one, each brutal impact driving the heavy figure backwards until he dropped into the lank grass and never moved again.

And it was over.

For a shocked moment Danny stood staring at his lethal handiwork while a thin, bluish thread of smoke was rising silently from his gun barrel.

Until a powerful arm suddenly wrapped around his shoulders. 'Kid,' Blain grinned, 'didn't I say you are the fastest thing these old eyes ever did see?' He burst into a wild derisive laugh. 'Did you see the look on old Winster's ugly face when he stopped that slug he knew had killed him? He was so—'

'*Why*, Blain?'

'Why what, kid?'

'All this.' Danny's gesture encompassed the dead. 'You knew I didn't have any cut coming, and so did they. Why did you push it when you knew what would happen? It was just an excuse to cut them out and get rid of them at the one time, wasn't it?'

Ketchell turned suddenly sober.

'I make the rules, kid. You're my brother and Blain Ketchell always watches out for his own, yessir. So, if I say you had a cut comin' that's how it is and no argument. *Sabe?*'

Mechanically, Danny began refilling the hot gun. 'You didn't fire a shot, Blain. Why not?'

Ketchell shrugged and grinned. 'Hell burn it, I didn't get a chance. Old Irby and Cull were all stretched out to dry before I could get into my stride!'

Danny seemed to take a long time with his gun. He dropped it back into the holster then wiped his hands against his shirt front as though they felt dirty. His face was furrowed, and when at last he looked at Blain his eyes seemed empty.

'Is that what you brought me along for, Blain? To do your killin' for you?'

'Now, what in tarnation gives you that notion, kid?' Ketchell said convincingly. 'You gunned them down and saved my life only for the one reason – you're double faster than any gun here today. Nothin' else.' He clapped him on the shoulder. 'But I understand how you feel. I was that way after the first time, but you'll get over it in a day or so. I did.'

So saying, he headed off for the horses.

'All right,' Danny sighed at length. 'Let's get busy. We need to get these two underground and be on our way. It's comin' on sundown.'

CHAPTER 4

THE KETCHELLS

The desert earth was hard and unyielding and it was gone midnight long before the final stones were stacked upon the outlaws' graves.

As the brothers rode away from the trees, Danny hipped around in the saddle for a last glimpse of the twin mounds lying in the moon shadow of the pines.

'Kid,' said Blain enthusiastically in an effort to shake the other out of his sombre mood, 'I just realized you and me have got us a great future. Think of it the two of us – the *Ketchells*! Why, hell, we'll carve out an empire together. We're not like these red-nosed and whey-faced walking dead you meet in every town and on every trail . . . gutless nobodies who bust their backs for fifty years over a shop counter or at the end of a plough, before dying broke. No sir. We'll just stand up tall on our hind legs and reach out and grab what we want and bury any man fool enough to try and stop us. Right, kid?'

'Sure, Blain.' the youth muttered, staring moodily at the mountains. 'That's right.'

Ketchell extracted one of his black cigars and lit up.

'Danny boy, it's time to tell you as how I got a big plan – biggest plan you ever heard of. Naturally I never told *them* about it,' he added, jerking a thumb back over his shoulder. 'And I won't even be tellin' you what it is for a spell neither. But it's somethin' big that will put you and me right in the chips – the big dinero! So, do you want to be in on that or do you want to quit? All up to you.'

'Sure I want in on it, Blain . . . you bet!'

'That's the spirit,' Ketchell smiled. 'See, you're feelin' better already. Bet you've stopped thinkin' about them dead fellers already . . . right?'

'Sure . . . forgotten.'

But Danny knew he wasn't forgetting anything, for those outlaws lying side by side in the cold black earth back there in the trees were haunting him already. He wondered if they always would . . . just as he wondered if he'd made the worst mistake of his life in allowing his brother to talk him into joining him in what he'd mistakenly figured would be a life of excitement and high times.

He couldn't shake the feeling that – bad as their reunion had proven to be already – there was worse to come. For his brother was proving to be nothing like the hero he'd always imagined him to be.

Emerson sat his saddle motionless in the sweating heat staring down at the graves.

Riding hard on Ketchell's trail he had encountered two abandoned horses some miles back, his first hint that trouble had overtaken the gang he hunted.

The juniper stand lay motionless in the panting noon silence all about him as he delayed to study the ugly rust-brown blood stains in the dust and grass. The footprints and those unmistakable furrows caused by dragging spurred boot-heels through the grass led all the way across to those two ugly mounds in the shade, telling their own grim story.

Danny's boots had walked away from those graves – but was the kid still wearing them?

Fighting off a chill feeling of dread he forced himself into action by firstly clearing away the stones upon the graves then digging his way down to the dead with a stubby saddle spade.

Winster and Tebbs seemed to rebuke him silently when finally uncovered. But he was unmoved. It wasn't Danny lying there with dirt on his dead face, and that was all that really counted.

Neither the heat nor hard labour burdened him now as he quickly refilled the graves and replaced the protecting stones. Holding his hat against his chest he mumured some quiet words before remounting and heeled the horse into a shuffling walk-trot.

He pushed south-west, riding into the afternoon.

Ahead, a smoky smudge against the deep blue sky, loomed the forbidding peaks of the Sangre de Cristos – the Blood of Christ mountains. He let the horse find its own best pace in the heat as he travelled on, a solitary horseman kicking a faint spiral of dust upwards into an immense and empty sky.

Topping out a low hill he caught a glimpse of the faraway town of Silver, seemingly suspended above the earth upon a shimmering blanket of heat.

To the south and running east past the mountains

lay the true desert, stretching to infinity. Briefly surveying the dried brush that led to undulating brown dunes, he licked dry lips absently, hawked and spat.

And thought, one jerk on the reins and I could be heading directly into that desert.

A man could survive in that country if he knew it, could travel carefully and by night, hitting the small water-holes and the horse-trading outposts.

Inside a week he could have put that terrible landscape far behind himself to cross the border and remain lost forever in one of those squalid little sheep villages which dotted the high plains.

Sure, a man could lose himself in that country, and Emerson had tipped that Ketchell's trail might take him there. Yet he kept angling in a different direction like a man heading someplace in particular, not just running before the law.

So the horse miles stretched away behind and he kept the animal pointed towards the smudge of the far mountains while the sun burned a hole in his back.

Jack Emerson was a hardened lawman, trail-wise beyond his years and so was well aware that this pursuit might well lead him to his death. And yet he held no fear for whatever might greet him ahead, either on this side or beyond those grim hills. Such matters held no weight compared with the way he felt about young Danny and the brother who may have never been young, riding at Danny's side and leading him to . . . where?

Whenever his spirits threatened to ebb he forced himself to think of Carmel and her agony of waiting, never knowing if either husband or kid brother would return. He knew her burden must be tougher to bear than his own.

Yet even apart from that he also had his own deep need for wanting to reach Danny Ketchell before it was too late.

And thought – had the boy killed back there? If so, there was no way of knowing how he really felt about that right now.

He dismounted briefly at the spot where the blackened remains of a campfire identified his quarry's resting spot. As he stood fashioning a cigarette he studied the hoofprints studding the endless trail. The horses must be tiring under the brutal pace they were being put to, but then, so was his own. But, luckily, his high-grade black had a huge heart, and he was confident in its ability to last.

Back in the saddle again with the mountains showing clearer now, the heat haze was gone and the murderous orb of the sun was dipping low towards the western rim.

He put another three or four miles behind him before twilight eventually deepened into evening. A dry creek bed fringed by stunty and dusted willows loomed ahead, and he turned his prad towards it.

Time to rest up.

He watered the mount and fed it some corn he kept in a slicker in his bedroll, then pegged the slicker to the earth so that the corn lay in it as in a dish. He put the mount on a long rope that permitted it to forage amongst the sparse grasses without the burden of man or saddle.

Rustling up a small fire he cooked beans and washed them down with two mugs of Arbuckle's, the fine coffee ridding his mouth of the tightness caused by dust and sun. He scrubbed the utensils in yellow, creek-bed sand and packed them away.

He sprawled out full length with his head resting upon his war bag and cigarette burning fragrantly between his teeth as he watched the moon make its appearance over distant hills.

He flicked the butt away and cupped both hands behind his head, listening to the cropping of the horse, and somewhere off in the sparse willows came the tiny scufflings of a foraging rodent.

Then he slept the long night away without dreaming.

The black didn't show signs of playing out some until around noon. It had been hard going those last ten miles stretching over increasingly parched country, piñon and aspen only serving to break the monotony of the terrain occasionally.

And always the Sangres brooding down, remote and indifferent.

Emerson crossed a wide creek bed and the tracks he was following now abruptly diverged to follow the line of the bank. One mile on he branched off to climb an upland slope, passing ancient cottonwoods dreaming in their own pools of black shadow, until a faint patina of smoke stained the sky ahead and two meadowlarks shot into the sky at the sounds of his approach.

He drew his Colt .45 and kept on, a grim, bronzed man riding out his destiny.

A small mud village appeared upon the slopes – a mere scatter of adobe huts and a handful of gaunt chickens foraging in the dust. . . .

The stall standing hard by one hut held several swayback horses . . . but no sign of Danny's sorrel mare.

He stepped down and waited. Soon they appeared, a slatternly woman and a pretty girl in a red dress, with bare legs and taut golden breasts. She appraised him boldly and smiled yet his face remained blank. This was a manhunt and he was the hunter. No time for distractions.

He said, 'Where are the men?'

'What men?' the girl challenged, plainly miffed by his lack of interest.

He nodded to the older woman who'd emerged to eye him suspiciously.

'Two horsemen rode in here not long ago,' he stated. 'A man and a youth. Which way did they go?'

She shrugged. 'No s*abe.*'

'Where are your menfolk?'

'Dead,' came the flat reply. 'Killed by white-eyes long ago.'

CHAPTER 5

RAIL TO REO LEON

'Soledo,' Emerson said, leaning down. 'Such a beautiful name for a beautiful girl!' And she primped a little at the compliment despite her innate seriousness. 'Soledo, if you know anything at all about Ketchell, where he's headed, how many men he has with him, you must tell me. I want to reach him before he kills again. And he surely will kill.'

'I-I don't know if I should say anything. But Ramon. . . .'

'Ramon?'

'My brother. He is but a boy.'

'He went with the others?' Jack demanded.

When this drew no response he spoke more forcefully. 'That man Ketchell is an outlaw, a *fugitivo*. He robbed the bank at Hudson and killed men there. Since then he has murdered the two outlaws who rode with him. If your men have gone off with him they'll never return to this place but will either die under the guns of the law or be slain by Ketchell. They are walking dead men.'

His words caused the woman to pale slightly, but raised a sharp intake of breath from another in the group.

'That is a lie!' this woman accused.

'It's the truth. I was sheriff of the town and I've followed them to this place. I saw the bodies of the men he killed and I expect to find more if I don't catch up with him fast.'

The woman studied him intently, dark eyes shrewd and speculating now.

'Why do you follow such men alone?' she wanted to know. 'It seems that if any shall die it will be you. You wear no badge so why should you be so brave?'

'I ain't brave but someone's got to stop this killer. He's a mad dog and nobody is safe while he's on the loose. If you ever want to see your man again you'd better tell me how many went with him and where they've headed.'

He saw the woman's eyes turn secretive and sensed she would reveal nothing even before she replied, 'You waste your time, gringo. I know nothing. That is what I tell the others, this is what I now tell you.'

His eyes narrowed sharply. 'Others? What others?'

'The *policia*.' She gestured towards the north. 'They came this morning. We tell them nothing so they ride on their way.'

'Police? You mean . . . Texas Rangers?'

'*Sí.*' A touch of contempt edged her voice.

Emerson was baffled. What in Hades' name was a Ranger company doing out here? The only reason that made sense was that they were also hunting Ketchell. He already knew the killer was the current full-time obsession of one Captain Will Calice.

'This *hombre*,' he said urgently, 'the leader of the Rangers, was he short, with big shoulders . . . a strong man with a beard?'

'*Sí.* So, now you go?'

'Damn right I go. But first, what route did the Rangers take? Which way?'

She paused momentarily then shrugged resignedly. 'They go south.' Her tone grew sharp. 'I do not like that *hombre*, that Calice. He has the look of a man without heart or mercy. I suspect he takes pleasure in hunting men like animals, that he would do so even if he were not paid.'

He didn't disagree. It wasn't hard to envision Calice storming into the little village, ranting and bullying. He was one mean sonova, and yet a ruthless and committed enemy of lawbreakers wherever he found them.

'You're wrong about Calice,' he said. 'But that's not important.' He tipped his hat. '*Adios.*'

The villagers stood around in silence as he led his horse away through the scattered mud-and-straw huts. As he mounted, the girl in the red dress came running after him.

'Señor!'

He looked down at her, momentarily distracted by just how lovely she was with clean-cut, regular features and an air of animal vitality. The dress was cut low, revealing the full firmness of her breasts.

'Yeah?'

'Is it true what you say about this *hombre* who shot his own *compañeros*?'

'Damn right it is. Why?'

She bit her lip and frowned back at the others. The villagers stood watching them now. She returned her attention to him.

'No man would be safe riding with such a one as

that.' It sounded both like a statement and a query.

'You're right about that,' he affirmed, thinking of Danny.

Again she hesitated, wringing her hands as she stared past him at the bleak mountains. She plainly had something on her mind. He wondered if it might be Ketchell.

Then, 'Soledo!'

It was the woman he'd spoken to who'd called. She moved a little towards them to stand frowning darkly at the girl, hostile and suspicious.

'Soledo!'

The woman had raised her voice and her tone this time was a command.

'Quickly!' he urged.

Her words came tumbling in a sudden rush. 'Ketchell talked them all into it – Ramon, Miguel Escopas . . . *idiotas*! He promised he would make them rich and they believed it. I told them he lied but he has the silver tongue and they went with him . . . rode off to die. Men like Ketchell are meant to die that way . . . but not Ramon . . . nor the young one with the beautiful eyes and the walk of a lion. . . .'

'Danny?' he guessed.

'*Sí* . . . Danny. We talked he and I long into the night. He was so beautiful and—'

'Where? Where in hell did they go? Did Ketchell say?'

'Danny told me . . . Reo Leon.'

'How—?'

Too late. The woman reached the girl and seized her roughly by the arm.

'Go!' she commanded him shrewishly. 'You are not welcome here!'

'*Adios*, Soledo,' he saluted.

'*Vaya con Dios*!' the girl gasped. And ignoring the woman dragging her away, added, '*Mi caballero.*'

He turned the horse about and rode out.

The gentle slope beyond the village was scarred and torn by the hoofs of many horses. He made no attempt to pick up the outlaw sign which would have been obliterated by the later passing of the Rangers.

He glanced back just the once before the village dropped from sight.

The angry woman had disappeared but he could still see the girl gazing after him, her dress a splash of crimson against the drab adobe of the *jacals*.

He waved but didn't know if she saw or not. Then he gigged the cayuse into a trot to be lost quickly in the enormity of the plains.

*

Emerson settled into the familiar rhythm of the ride. As he passed through the increasingly bleak and hostile south-west desert country he reflected on what the girl had told him.

There was, of course, no guarantee she had spoken the truth, and he didn't rule out the possibility that Ketchell could have coached her to spin a story in the event of her being questioned.

He shook his head stubbornly. No!

She *was* telling the truth, he was certain of it. This meant Ketchell had come to the village and and taken men away into the deeper south-west with him. That could only indicate he was preparing to strike again. But where? Reo Leon? That was what she had said and maybe he halfway believed her.

He recalled Reo Leon dimly as a sweltering adobe town many long miles beyond the Sangre de Cristos. It was a squalid, fetid hole upon the unmarked fringe of the dreaded Staked Plains. Hard to believe that Ketchell might have any sensible reason for making such a punishing ride out to that butt-end of no place. . . .

It didn't add up.

He pushed the horse a little harder now, eager to catch up with Calice. Should those mule-stubborn Rangers run Ketchell down there would be gunplay for sure, and ruthless Calice would have no compunction in shooting down that entire bunch – Danny included.

It was mid afternoon before he sighted the tell-tale smudge of distant dust rising against the rapidly nearing mountains. The Rangers would be slowed down by their pack-animals and equipment, he figured. He estimated them to be between five and six miles ahead.

He studied the black's drooping neck, realized he would have to spell the animal or run the risk of burning him out.

Reluctantly he swung off for the cover of a rocky mesa where loomed two huge rocks which had teetered almost off-balance for centuries without actually toppling. These provided excellent shade and there was even a hint of coolness in the shadows.

Squatting cross-legged upon the ground he sipped sparingly from the canteen and studied the surrounding mountains. He glanced at the sun to figure out the time and finally looked back trail.

He instantly cursed and jumped erect.

For out there was a growing smudge of cloud to the south-west and upon the horizon rim a ridge of thunderheads were churning and billowing into the sky. Even as he gaped and cussed, the mutter of distant thunder rumbled in the distance.

Storm coming!

He swore viciously and the weary horse jerked its head at the sound of his voice.

Without delay he flung saddle and gear across the animal's still-sweating back and mounted up. With a final disgruntled look back he slapped the lines and started off.

He hadn't figured on rain on account of the weather being so hot, and his cursing grew more colourful as the horse broke into a weary canter.

For rain would obliterate all sign in this dust country. Trailing, if possible at all, would be a laborious process of searching for overturned pebbles or the odd hoofprint in a rare patch of clay that somehow managed to survive the rain. He was a hard man to depress but the weight across his shoulders seemed to grow heavier with every mile he put behind him now.

The Rangers' dust grew clearer and he could envision the invective Calice would have been directing up at that threatening sky.

Now a fast shadow came racing across the face of the plains to envelop the lone rider swiftly before rushing on towards the mountains as tumbling masses of cloud half-covered the sky and quickly engulfed the sun.

The thunder crashed louder and lightning worked in the darkening clouds. A sudden gust of hot wind surged over him and went on to engulf a distant wooded hillside, rippling shapes across its growth like massive fingers.

He hauled on his slicker and was fastening the buttons across his chest when the storm hit.

Initially just a spatter of big, solitary drops of ice-cold water which drummed noisily against his slicker for several minutes then, within seconds, the entire world was obliterated by teeming torrents of rain, the thunder deafening to the ear. He hunched his shoulders and tried to ignore icy water running down his spine.

The storm lashed and raged for a full half-hour and then was gone as abruptly as it had come, the receding clouds now engulfing the face of the distant ranges.

He realized he was less than a mile from the Ranger company when visibility cleared, saw that they had drawn up under the lee of a mesa to wait out the storm's fury whereas he'd kept going.

Heads lifted in surprise as he approached.

There were ten men in the group with roughly twice that many horses, most of the animals runty Mexican mustangs so favoured by many Rangers in the force.

A lookout bawled a yell of recognition and started towards him. The man was not young but was robust of physique with a massive head, iron-grey beard and whiskers, his skin burned a rich brown by the Texas sun.

'Howdy there, Will,' Emerson replied, swinging to ground and reaching for the outstretched hand.

'Emerson! What in tarnation are you doing out here?' Calice's voice was deep and resonant, ideally suiting that powerful frame.

'Why, same as you, Will. Hunting Ketchell.'

'What?'

Before Emerson could reply, one of his men called, 'Coffee's ready, sir!'

'Huh? Oh ... very well,' Calice responded. 'Come have some hot Arbuckle's, Jack. Then you can tell me just why in hell's name you're chasing that arrogant buzzard.'

The two hunkered down upon a gear pile and over the welcome if bitter brew Emerson related the events leading up to their meeting, carefully avoiding any mention of Danny.

When he was about through, he added, 'But how come you got going after Ketchell so fast? I sent you a wire at Zebulon after the dust-up in Hudson.'

The Ranger rose and began pacing to and fro,

hands locked behind.

'I was over in Silver when you sent that wire, having got there just before it arrived. They'd sent it on from Zebulon. I'd tracked Ketchell up from the south but he'd lost me.'

He paused to emit a blistering obscenity before continuing.

'Never figured they'd make a try for Hudson, y'know. Well, when I got your wire I got in touch with Hudson. You were already out after the bunch but they were able to tell me the gang had headed west.'

He halted before Emerson and wagged a big finger.

'I hunkered down and finally decided I wasn't going to be led up any dead-end by that sonova, nosir. As you know I've been camped on Ketchell's trail for quite a spell now and I'm getting wise to some of his tricks as well as finding out places where he's likely to hang his hat. He's been back to that village that you saw, and he has some pards there . . . two stupid *paisanos*. I knew this, so when I found out what had happened I took an educated guess and figured he just might head there.' He slapped his chest proudly. 'And I was right.'

'Yeah, OK,' conceded Jack, tossing the dregs from his cup and rising. 'So – where in the Sam

Hill is he now?'

Calice glared up at the sky and cursed luridly. 'We *had* him!' he boomed, turning heads. 'And then it rained!'

'Rained?' Jack was tempted to grin, but thought better of it. Instead, he related what he'd picked up from the Mexican girl but Calice seemed unimpressed.

'Hah!' he spat contemptuously. 'She's just like the rest of that unwashed bunch. Any one of them would false swear their own mother up on to the gibbet for a peso. No, you can forget all about that lead, son.'

'I felt she was on the level. Matter of fact, thinking on it now I'm sure she was telling me the truth.'

'Look, Emerson,' the big man enunciated slowly, 'you've been a lawman far too long to be taken in by any *paisano* wench. Why under the sun would she tell you where Ketchell and the villagers went? *Why?*'

'She said her brother was in the bunch. Said she was afraid he'd finish up like Tebbs and Winster. That's the reason she gave me.'

Calice muttered disgustedly and recommenced his pacing, shoulders hunched aggressively and lower lip protruding.

'Prepare to break camp!' he bawled, propping suddenly. He swung to face Emerson. 'All right, goddamnit, just say for the moment she was telling the truth. Why would Ketchell go to Reo Leon?'

'Don't know.'

'Nor do I. That dump is just a rat's hole of Mexes, *paisanos*, loafing Injuns, rum-pot whites and throat-slitting crooks living on the edge of hell. So you give me one reason why a high-stepper like Ketchell would go there,' challenged Calice.

'Can't. But I'm still not changing my mind. The way Ketchell's moving tells me he's got to be heading south-west for a special place for a specific reason. He's recruiting a new bunch and that says he's got a job in mind. I reckon that could be at Reo Leon,' Jack responded.

'Buffalo dust!'

'You got a better explanation?'

'Reckon I have. I happen to know there's a gold shipment making for Ford City west of the Sangre de Cristos. That sounds more like his kind of bait.'

'He was heading for the mountains, I keep telling you,' Jack argued.

'Shortest track to Ford City if you've got the guts for that mountain crossing.'

'The Army always posts a horse-guard with those shipments from Ford City. You don't figure

Ketchell would be loco enough to take on the Army, do you?'

'That guard adds up to just four cavalrymen strong, Emerson. Ketchell could drum up double that strength without even trying, then plan the raid down to the last detail. Only thing, this time I'll be waiting for him.'

'You're planning to ride to Ford City?'

'Right. And I'd be pleasured to have you ride with me and—' Calice broke off sharply, suddenly suspicious. 'Say, I didn't ask. What in tarnation are you dogging him this far for?'

'He robbed the Hudson Bank. So, it's my job.'

'You're not wearing a badge.'

'Right. I calculated I might be away days, maybe weeks. So I handed over to my deputy until I got back.'

Calice scowled suspiciously. 'You sure there's nothing personal in all this? I mean, on account of Ketchell being your wife's brother, maybe?'

'No. I just aim to get back the money he stole.'

Calice appeared satisfied. 'Well, we're about to push on. You riding with us?'

'No. I'm heading direct for Reo Leon.'

Calice glanced at his men lined up on their horses now. 'All right. But if you run foul of Ketchell, contact me at Ford City. He's more than a handful for any one man.'

'We'll see.'

They shook hands and the Ranger took the reins from one of his men and swung up. The riders waited for his signal but he again turned to Jack.

'I nearly forgot, son. There's a shipment coming to Austin from Montana shortly by way of Reo Leon. The officer in charge is Lieutenant Tiddrick, a good man. Look him up if they come through while you're in that dirty town.' He made a wry grimace. 'You'll find him a welcome change from the citizens of Reo.'

Emerson touched hat brim with fingertips and Calice heeled his mount away.

'Company Seven – *forward – ho*!'

Jack stood motionless for some time afterwards, a solitary figure on the rim of the mesa watching the Rangers go, the reappearing sun striking points of fire from rifles and harness. Calice waved back just once as they swung away from the made trail, heading for Ford City.

Fashioning and then firing up a brown-paper quirley, Emerson shortly filled leather himself and took the trail that would take him over the inhospitable Sangre de Cristos. With the mountains behind him he would then continue onwards across vast and empty miles of badlands until at last, if mount and good fortune didn't fail him, he would raise the infamous desert hell town of Reo Leon.

CHAPTER 6

RED LEON

Blain Ketchell leaned lazily against the crumbling wall of the *jacal* with thumbs hooked in his cartridge belt, grinning across at Danny.

'You fixin' to wear the Colt right away, kid? I swear I never did see a man pamper a six-shooter like you in all my days.'

Danny hunkered on his boot-heels and glanced up, boyish features sober.

'The thing is about a gun ... you never know when you might be called upon to use it.' He glanced across at the men lounging in the deep shade, his lip curling in contempt. 'Most especially with scum like that around.'

'Don't let 'em faze you, kid. They're on our side, remember?'

'Yeah, our side.' Danny sounded bitter. He fell silent again and continued polishing the weapon with a strip of soft cloth as Ketchell fired up a fat stogie before strolling off.

The gang had camped amongst the crumbling remains of an adobe village sprawled across a scrabble-rocked hillside overlooking the sun-stricken desert outpost of Reo Leon.

Some long-ago landslide that had come roaring down from the granite mesa above had left this ancient town half-buried and deserted. Piñon, thorny cactus and brown patches of maguey dotted the slopes with just two hardy cottonwoods left to afford a little sparse shelter for the travel-stained party.

Drifters and hardcases, the added riders had been recruited from three *paisano* villages they'd passed through, two this side of the Sangre de Cristos and the third beyond.

Danny's thoughts drifted back to that first, desolate desert town with its rank air of poverty and hopelessness. He thought it odd that such a hog-pen place should be the home to that lovely olive-skinned girl with raven hair and a voice like silk.

He scowled at the men nearby, his gaze focusing upon the skinny and pock-marked Ramon for long moments, his scowl cutting even deeper.

'*Take care of Ramon, Danny,*' she had begged of him. '*He's only a boy.*'

He smiled humourlessly. From what he had seen of Ramon with his endless griping, his bragging and posturing and his slinking scavenger manner, he reckoned the best and fairest way to take care of him could be a .45 slug where it would do the most good.

But maybe that assessment could be justifiably applied to them all, he mused sourly, for virtually all the other badmen shared some or most of Ramon's ugly traits and habits.

'Ready, kid?'

He glanced up. Blain was now toting two sets of shabby coveralls along with hats that were equally battered and incredibly dirty. He'd also donned a luxurious false moustache which, as Danny was forced to admit, provided a convincing if ludicrous disguise.

'We goin' in now?' He came erect, dropping the gleaming gun into its cutaway holster.

'Uh-huh.' Blain proffered a set of coveralls. 'Get yourself into these. We want to pass off as the crummiest lookin' *hombres* ever seen in this lousy town, and that will sure take some doing.'

Danny took the garments and both busied themselves fixing their disguises. Danny's pants were too long so he rolled them up at the cuffs, allowing them to hang sloppily over his fancy boot-tops.

'Them boots of yours don't look much like a bum's to me,' Blain commented.

'Nobody's goin' to be lookin' at my boots.'

'Maybe so, maybe not. Better change out of 'em.'

'The hell I—' He halted abruptly. Ketchell's stare was suddenly cold and hard. So he forced a grin, altered his tone. 'These boots were given me, Blain. I got a feelin' they bring me luck.'

Ketchell deliberated a long moment, finally shrugged. 'Hell, maybe they do at that. OK, leave 'em on.' He spun a battered hat across to him. 'Anyway, once you get that disguise on even I wouldn't know you.'

Danny realized the change in them both was convincing the moment flashy trail clothes and eye-catching six-shooters were engulfed beneath the rag-tag of ancient denim coveralls, with sorry hats replacing sombreros. Behind his drooping moustache, Blain looked a dead-beat to the boot-straps ... doubly so when he hunched his shoulders and began limping up and down with the shuffling gait of a weary old bum.

'The *señor* can spare a peso for the sick old man?' he whined, and Danny chuckled.

As others joined in the laughter, Ramon crossed to the brothers with his phoney grin.

'We going into the town too?' he asked hopefully.

'No. Us two are goin' in to stake out the place. Danny and me can handle it between us.'

Ramon scowled. 'It is a long time since I was in a big town. I would find much pleasure in some brandy – and maybe a *señorita*?'

'After the job, Ramon. Plenty of time for fun then,' he was told.

The man began to object again until cut off by Danny.

'Why don't you just shut up?' he snapped. 'Even I don't know what's goin' on, so why should you?'

The youths hadn't gotten along from the get-go, and tension had deepened over the passing days. Yet this was the first time their enmity had surfaced, and Blain was quick to cut in.

'Break it off!' he growled. 'You'll likely get all the fightin' you crave plenty soon I'm thinkin' – mebbe more than you want.' He turned to Danny, and grunted, 'Let's dust, kid.'

With that he headed off to where the horses stood dozing in the shade. As Danny made to follow Ramon muttered something under his breath, causing him to prop and turn sharply.

'What did you say?' he demanded.

'Nothin' . . . vamoose – gringo!'

Lightning fast, Danny threw an overhand right that caught Ramon in the mouth and drew crimson.

'Danny – goddamnit!' bawled Blain, and whirling, came running back.

Before he could reach the pair, Danny had ducked a wild swing then sledged a right rip into the belly. This was followed fast by a jolting hook to the side of the head that knocked his adversary off his feet to tumble face down in the dirt.

Instantly Blain seized him by the shoulders, reefing him away as others went to the dazed Ramon's aid. Danny felt his sudden anger draining away even before his brother opened up on him.

'You damn hothead! What in hell are you tryin' to do?'

Danny refused to respond but stalked off to his mount. Ramon had recovered some by this but still looked sick. The *vaqueros* supporting him glared across at the Americans but his brother just kept silent and simply shrugged then motioned to him to mount up before crossing to his own cayuse.

'They're just yearlin's feelin' their oats,' he commented laconically, and kicked his mount into a walk-trot, with Danny following.

'Sorry about that—' Danny began, but got no further.

'Hell, don't sweat, kid.'

'You – you ain't mad?'

' 'Course not,' Blain replied, raising his voice to be heard above the clatter of hoofs on broken stone. 'They're nothin' but a bunch of stupes that'll do as I tell 'em when and if I need them. Even so, you better be careful about swingin' punches thataway.' He winked. 'Hands like ours are valuable tools of trade. Use a gunbutt next time.'

They laughed easily and Danny knew that riding with Blain and living by their own rules in the wild lands had to be about as good as things could get – or close, anyway.

Yet he found the brief excitement a welcome relief following the monotony of the days it had taken to cross the Sangre de Cristos. In truth he'd been feeling low ever since Tebbs and Winster were killed.

The intervening time since had been largely marked by long hours in the saddle with heat, flies and dust every mile sapping everybody's energy and spirits – all but Blain's, anyway.

For the first time he'd come to realize fully what his older brother was really made of during that ride. He glanced across at him now – still ridiculous in that labourer's rig yet as always sitting easy in the saddle – impressive, untiring and always-durable Blain.

He understand more completely now just how the other had been able to elude the law for so long. It would take some special breed ever to bring Blain Ketchell down, he mused. Yet that thought instantly conjured up the image of the one man he knew who just might be equal to such a challenge. Well – almost.

Jack Emerson was his name.

'No!' He protested aloud, looking guiltily ahead at his brother. *Nobody* could match Blain. Never and no way!

'Hey, there she is, kid!'

His brother's voice jolted him back to the present. 'Huh? What's that, Blain?'

The other made a sweeping gesture as they emerged from the jaws of a pass to confront the panoramic vista of a sluggish brown stream with a sprawling mud city lining its banks down in the river valley below.

'Reo Leon, kid, end of the trail!' his brother laughed. 'Reckon you expected somethin' flashier, huh?'

'Well, it sure enough ain't flash.'

Clattering swiftly down the stony trail they eventually approached a bridge slung across the turgid river. Huddled mud huts sprawled away on all sides, squat adobe ovens that resembled a colony of outsized beehives.

Dull-eyed men and women squatted upon low stoops waiting for any breath of air the gathering dusk might bring. They gazed dully at the passing gringo gunmen with little interest. Half-naked children, already plagued by the lethargy that came from bad eating habits and a hostile climate, watched the riders balefully and refused to give way on the street, forcing them to ride around them while they stood cursing and spitting into the dry dust between bare feet.

Welcome to Helltown!

Maybe he shouldn't have chosen the shorter of the two trails that would take him where he wanted to go?

So Emerson's thinking was running as he stealthily removed his broad-brimmed hat and placed it upon the earth at his side. Only then, spread out full length in the dust, did he run the risk of raising his head above his protecting white boulder to snatch a quick look to the south-west.

And saw them still making in his direction as they had been doing ever since he'd first awakened from an uneventful night's sleep to glimpse feathered horsemen invading the valley.

He'd known at first sight they were Indians, but not what kind. And out here in the no-man's-land of the vast and hostile Sundance Valley, accurately identifying the breed of any Injun could often prove the difference between life and death.

His heart began to trot in his chest when his lips formed the name, 'Comanche war party by the looks – wouldn't a man just *know* it!'

In his younger days Emerson had fought Quahada Comanches during the last of the great break-outs. He had buried buffalo hunters who had been skinned alive and roasted, and there were still times when a man's imagination conjured up their remembered screams which could throb like an exposed nerve long after their graves had been covered over them. . . .

'Quit that line of thinking!' he muttered aloud, and snatching up his rifle, proceeded to do the only thing he could as a lone white man sharing one small patch of the West with a party of twenty or maybe thirty Comanches, all painted up for war and heading in his general direction.

He burrowed out of sight under a deadfall tree and began praying the horse would stay quiet in the draw where he'd peg-roped it to feed.

Soon, with one ear pressed hard against the grassy earth, he heard the low stutter of approaching hoofbeats. Reluctantly, he began reliving memories of a life lived always on the edge of danger as scout, hunter, occasional pathfinder for the Army – and now, what?

A wild howl was followed by the unmistakable rumble of a large number of horses breaking into a gallop. There were shouts and loud hooting as the hoofbeats drew swiftly closer and he knew that somehow, despite all the cunning he'd put into selecting this shelter in danger country, they must have sighted something he'd overlooked – something maybe that could cost him both his hair and his life!

Fatalistically, he prepared himself for the inevitable. He would stand facing the enemy and give him all he had with both guns . . . until. . . .

He was on the verge of doing just that when he realized that the rumble of hoofbeats, although still loud and far too damned close for comfort, seemed more distant than before. Sweat running from his brow stung his eyes as he forced himself to lie motionless in the brush to hold on and wait – seemingly for an eternity yet in reality no longer than a minute. Then he knew his ears hadn't deceived him. The hoofbeats were indeed fading, going fast now.

The thirty seconds that followed seemed more like an hour before his heartbeat began to slow of its own accord and he knew they were really gone – yet he was veteran enough to give it another half-minute before he dared move a muscle.

He warily raised his head above cover to glimpse a cavalry charge of painted savages a mile to the south-east boisterously in pursuit of the blurred brown bulk of a honey bear streaking desperately for the river.

He stood upright and stared up at the precious sky, then set off at the run to recover his horse.

It took a long time for him to quit sweating and finish praying.

'Some town, eh, kid?' Ketchell remarked sardonically.

'Yeah,' Danny answered, still uncertain as to what they were doing here.

The street led directly into the plaza where the oil lamps of evening were already making everything a little brighter as the short desert twilight deepened into night.

Citizens moved unhurriedly along the walks and across the square. Mexicans, Apaches, *paisanos*, Pueblos, whites, breeds – they'd seen them all by the time they reined in at the long hitchrail out front of a white-painted cantina.

Danny glanced questioningly at Blain who jerked his head towards the cantina, then led the way in through the slatted doors.

The same atmosphere of decay and disillusion they'd encountered on the street prevailed indoors. Card players with sombreros shadowing their faces beneath smoking oil lamps ... greasy pasteboards sliding over felt-covered tables ... drinkers lining the bar ... a dozen dialects merging into one low murmuring buzz and sloe-eyed girls glancing at the travel-stained newcomers and stifling bored yawns.

Had he ever struck a meaner-looking town? The answer just had to be no.

He trailed his brother across to the bar, Blain moving lightly despite exhaustion.

A bug-eyed and oily-haired barkeep silently raised eloquent black eyebrows at them.

'What you got?' Ketchell asked.

'*Aguardiente* or beer.'

'*Aguardiente*,' said Ketchell, and the bartender splashed pale rum into dark glasses.

They chinked glasses and drank silently, Danny almost gagging on that first harsh taste but quickly relaxing as he felt the warmth tingle his blood. Blain tossed his shot down at a gulp and turned back to the bartender.

'Good liquor,' he declared. 'Give me a bottle.'

The man glanced at their ragged rig dubiously but beamed amiably again when Blain waved a ten-spot under his nose. He quickly produced a bottle of rum and drew the cork. He picked up the bill and had turned to his cash box when Blain dropped a hand on his arm.

'Keep the change,' he said, 'I got plenty.' He turned to other drinkers close by. 'I'm treating, boys. So line up and order your poison.'

Danny almost laughed at the expression of comic surprise that crossed so many faces. Nobody ever treated here; it wasn't that kind of place.

'Those boys too,' Blain said, indicating the roughnecks at a nearby table. His big smile encompassed everybody. 'C'mon, pour them out and we'll drink them up, I'm making it that kind of a night.'

The saloon lizards needed no second bidding and soon a relaxed and boozy atmosphere prevailed. Danny sat watching and listening intently as his brother took charge and boosted everyone's flagging spirits with the force of his energy and personality.

He soon realized that Blain was subtly pumping the locals for information, but about what he couldn't be sure. The conversation touched on crops, hard times, the heat, horses and women and his brother seemed to deal with each impartially.

Until eventually the talk focused on horses and Danny pricked his ears.

He gathered there was rumoured to be a herd of horses due to reach Reo Leon almost any time now. Blain told them he was a wrangler looking for work and kept them talking on the topic of the horses, and learned plenty. He found out just how many animals were due and how many Rangers were expected to accompany the mob. One deadbeat revealed that the horses were bound for the station at Austin and predicted how long the riders might be expected to stop over in town. He also heard where the animals would be corralled, virtually everything they'd wanted to find out. Yet he handled his enquiries so easily and politely that Danny felt certain none suspected just how much he was actually pumping out of them.

By then Danny felt certain he understood what

had brought them here to Reo Leon, but this only caused him to feel even more confused than before.

He glanced up as the batwings were noisily banged open and two men entered. They halted just inside the doorway to glower around at the drinkers before focusing upon Blain himself.

They traded nods then came forward.

Both were Mexicans, one fat and bloated, the other lean and nondescript, both coated with days of untidy beard stubble. Each wore a star on his vest. It seemed that Reo Leon law was as much on the rough-and-ready side as the town itself.

The pair halted before Ketchell's group and the fat one addressed him roughly.

'You! You are a stranger here!'

He made this sound like an accusation, but Ketchell simply turned to him with a lazy grin.

'*Sí* Señor Sheriff. We, my buddy Haji and me, just arrived. We came in from Twin Bells. We're *vaqueros*, looking for work.'

'Uh-huh.' It was hard to tell if the fat man believed him or not. Yet after a moment he shrugged, apparently satisfied. 'Very well, but mind you observe the law. We have some very bad *hombres* coming to Reo Leon.'

'Heck, I can easy believe that,' Ketchell assured,

shooting a sly wink at Danny. 'Er, Señor Sheriff, I know you are on duty, but maybe you would care to share a drink with us?'

'Well' – the grubby lawman deliberated, glancing thirstily at the bottle – 'maybe just the one. . . .'

And Ketchell and Danny traded smiles. This breed of law would pose few problems.

CHAPTER 7

THE BIG DARK

Before the batwings had ceased swinging the sheriff had downed his first glass of Mother's Ruin gin. He belched noisily.

'Another, *señor*?' suggested Ketchell, already pouring.

'*Gracias.* Your very good health, *señor.*'

It continued in that vein over the next hour, and so absorbed did Danny become in enjoying his brother's masquerade that for the first time he felt free of the depression which had been weighing him down ever since the gunfight.

Once Blain felt he'd won the confidence of the local badgeman he'd quickly steered the conversation around to the horses due to arrive here any time now. A grinning Danny could see that Blain was now truly enjoying his masquerade, and not once did he slip out of the role he was playing, that of an innocent *paisano vaquero*.

At last Blain had all he needed and rose from his stool, swaying slightly and hiccupping when he spoke again.

'Señor lawmen, I must leave you now but will you do me the honour of finishing this bottle – at my expense. It's an honour to drink with such *caballeros*!'

His drinking companions were genuinely drunk, whereas he was sober as a judge. There followed handshakes and backslapping and flowery farewells – south of the border style.

'*Adios*!' called the sheriff as they made for the batwings. '*Vaya con Dios!*'

The brothers went through the swinging doors together and crossed the gallery.

The plaza was all but deserted now, just the huddled form of an old bum leaning against an adobe wall and a solitary lady of the evening wending her unsteady way homewards the only signs of life.

And once again both were aware of it – that sinister quality in the very air here that seemed to suggest secrecy, danger and a jittery uncertainty wherever one ventured in sordid Reo Leon. It was as if drinkers and stumble bums and three-time-losers nursed some deep secret which gun-toting gringos were not privy to.

Yet even if such a secret did exist they weren't interested, for they had more than enough to occupy themselves without adding to it.

Once clear of the *placita*, Blain Ketchell quit stumbling, threw his shoulders back and laughed, the abrupt sound ringing in the empty street and causing a hound to yelp in sudden alarm. He winked at Danny with a big grin, teeth gleaming whitely.

'Ever see anything like that, kid? That lawdog, I mean. I met the fraud two years ago when I passed through here last, but I was togged out as a half-breed Comanche that day. He was stupid then and sure hasn't changed any since.'

Danny nodded, marvelling at the other's ability to play a drunk so convincingly.

'So, what now?' he slurred.

'Just you tag along with me. C'mon, I got to go check out something.'

Bustling with energy, Ketchell led the way confidently through sleeping, trash-littered back streets to eventually reach the open flats south of town.

Before them in the moonlight was to be seen a series of large corrals, some obviously recently built.

The two mounted up and circled the corrals for a spell before Ketchell drew rein and sat his saddle surveying the scene before him.

'Uh-uh,' he muttered as if talking to himself after a time. 'One dead-set, sure-fire big cinch . . . to be sure.'

'You wouldn't be planning on stealing those Rangers' horses, by any chance?' Danny asked, half-excited, half-alarmed.

'On target, boy. Forty blood horses from up Montana way. Worth a mint on any market. I've travelled many a risky mile to get to stand here looking at the finest bunch of blood horses any man will ever see, and it was worth every yard of it.'

Danny grinned, feeling his excitement. 'So, why didn't you let me in on this before?'

'Hadn't quite made up my own mind then. I first made the plans for this six months back when I was in these parts last, dealing with some of the weirdest fellers you'll ever see, low-life desert scum who want to rule from here to forever. And they'll most likely get to do just that once they come by these fine new army horses due here any day now—'

'But how'll they come by these here horses if—'

Ketchell tapped the side of his nose. 'Got all that covered, laddy buck. This rich and flashy dog pack wanted the finest animals money could buy and had the dinero to pay for them, so I set about organizing for them to get just what they wanted. It took time and a lot of shooting to find out just when and where these horses would be coming through, like I'd heard they would be. Well, they're here . . . and I know just how to steal 'em.'

Realizing he was dead serious, Danny sobered.

'But they belong to the goddamn Rangers now, man. Nobody ever takes nothing off *them*.'

'Never say never, kid. . . .'

Blain got a stogie smoking before continuing, his voice sounding powerful and confident in this deep Texas night.

'You see, the notion that anybody would even *dream* about lifting any bunch this size in this crummy hole – especially belonging to the Rangers – never occurred to anybody.' He paused to grin again. 'But of course they only *think* they know yours truly. And you know something that old Lard Guts the lawman told me? There'll be just four Rangers bringing them in, along with a few dumb cowboys. A cinch!'

His confidence was infectious, but Danny still

felt it all sounded one hell of a high-risk proposition. Yet he was careful not to let his scepticism show. Blain was no longer the hero he'd taken him to be and their time together had revealed his brother to be the most dangerous man he'd ever encountered. He knew he was afraid of him – and bitterly regretted joining up with him now.

Even so, there were things he still wanted to know. 'But what can you do with so many horses? And Ranger horses at that?'

Ketchell glanced away.

'I got me a market.'

It wasn't so much what was said as the way it sounded that sent a chill through the younger man. It was as if a door had opened upon a dark place only his brother knew of.

'Where is this market?' he persisted.

Blain swung on him, his face suddenly almost that of a stranger. 'Don't push me, kid. Not ever. I'll tell you when I reckon you're ready to know, not before. You got that straight in that bone head of yours?'

Without waiting for a response he whirled his mount and kicked it in the ribs.

'C'mon, we're getting back to camp!' he yelled and raked once with spur to send the gelding leaping away to circle the corrals before breaking into a full gallop upon gaining the open country beyond.

With a puzzled shake of the head, Danny slapped the reins and followed at the run.

'*I got me a market.*'

The words buzzed in his skull as he trailed his brother out across the rickety little bridge then up along the climbing trail that led back to the camp. He squinted ahead at the dim figures of horse and rider and couldn't help shaking his head, thinking, 'Forty blood horses – worth a fortune. But who'd have that sort of money to hell and gone out here?'

The camp lay in darkness when they arrived, and Blain headed off directly to his bedroll in one of the deserted *jacals* without another word.

Danny sat smoking in silence for a long time beneath a huge old cottonwood, gazing out beyond the feeble lights of Reo Leon towards the immensity of the Staked Plains sprawled vastly in eternal and mysterious silence beneath an outlaw moon.

He found himself calling to mind strange and blood-curdling tales of these Plains and their sinister denizens whom some insisted ruled far out there in the back of the beyond. He'd heard stories, maybe fanciful, of the hideous fate awaiting any man who dared venture too far to the south-west of this bend in the river in what some old-timers referred to for some strange reason as The Land Of Comancheria.

It was almost daylight before he fell into an uneasy sleep.

Jack Emerson entered Reo Leon in the dead of night, the hoofs of his dusty black echoing hollowly in empty streets.

He passed beneath a low-burning street light, the glow briefly illuminating his face, revealing gaunt, stubbled cheeks and weary eyes.

A beggar arose from deeper shadows and whined a plea for money but Jack passed on by without even a glance.

He didn't rein in until reaching the plaza.

A diffused yellow light shone from a shambling building with an unpainted iron roof – obviously the hotel.

He climbed down stiffly and with war bag over his shoulder walked from the tie-rack and mounted the steps to pass through the creaking doors.

A musty stink of decay and neglect assailed him as he stood surveying the shabby foyer: battered chairs, weather-stained walls, a broken window and a life-sized portrait of Sam Houston hanging in pride of place above the desk.

A man in a deep chair snored behind the desk, a crumpled and grimed figure with a red drinker's nose and a dribble of saliva upon his chin.

Emerson turned on his heel and returned to the plankwalk, the air of this losers' town seeming almost sweet after the turgid atmosphere indoors.

He paused for a time, momentarily undecided in his weariness. The hope of snatching even a few hours in a real bed had disappeared and there was but the one alternative – sleep out beneath the stars. Again.

So he remounted and rode from the plaza and kept on until he was a mile out of town on the banks of the sluggish brown river. He reined in by a clump of piñon and sat wearily in the saddle for some time . . . testing.

No mosquitoes.

Good enough.

He got down and unsaddled. Removing the horse's harness he substituted a long rope for it which he knotted to a tree close by. Too weary even to unpack his bedroll he simply sprawled upon the worn-out grama grass beneath the tree, his saddle as a pillow.

Within moments he was asleep and didn't

waken until the hot sun was burning his upturned face.

Stiffly he rose and stretched then set about chores which had become routine.

A short time later found him shaved and fed and brushing the horse. He was soon halfway through his first tin mug of Arbuckle's coffee with a skillet of bacon crisping over a small fire.

The weariness was gone and there were no real aches or stiffness to bother him as had been the case during his first few days out of Hudson. He studied his hands. They were burned brown and the palms were callused and hard from the reins. Maybe he'd been out of shape a little upon setting out on this odyssey, but that was no longer the case. He reckoned it to be around ten oclock by the sun as he munched bacon and took his first good look at Reo Leon by daylight.

What had appeared to him as a totally depressing place by night appeared almost worse under the harsh light of day.

Smoke tendrils wisped thinly from ramshackle *jacals* and he glimpsed women moving sluggishly about their chores, washing clothes in iron pots and occasionally screaming obscenities at unheeding children.

He grinned humourlessly. Their lives had to be

miles safer than his own, but he still knew which he would prefer.

Few men were to be seen as yet. Likely far too early for the nocturnal males of Reo Leon to be abroad, if he was any judge.

He grinned as he packed up, recalling Will Calice's description of the town. 'A poverty-stricken hole with a climate straight out of hell.' Sounded pretty accurate from what he had seen of it so far.

Riding off with the sluggish brown stream behind him he decided to undertake a proper daylight survey of the town before he would begin looking for the Ketchells. He'd not cut their sign since the day of the big storm but hadn't lost hope of finding them again here in Reo Leon.

His way took him to the south side of town where he saw the huge corrals waiting for the horses expected in from the north-west. Several men were putting the finishing touches to these structures and he swung down to yarn with them for a spell, learning that the mob was due to show up any time now.

He continued on, not really interested in horses. He had far more important things on his mind.

Roaming the outskirts until noon he returned to

the town to find himself a tolerable livery where he checked the horse, warning the bug-eyed proprietor against mishandling or neglect. Then to be doubly sure he paid twice the asking fee. A former female acquaintance had once accused him of caring more for this horse than her and he suspected that to be close to the truth.

Quitting the livery he reconnoitred the plaza and eventually reached the conclusion that about the only thing here that could possibly attract Blain Ketchell to Reo Leon had to be its tiny bank.

Yet when he stood before that unpainted plank-and-batten repository of the town's wealth, he was forced to change his mind. Plainly there wouldn't be enough cash here to warrant undertaking such a long and brutal journey for any big-time *bandido*.

The rickety bank stood but a short distance from the sheriff's office where a man sporting a rusted star sat on the front porch, hat tilted forwards against the glare.

This turned out to be the deputy, who, upon learning that the gringo stranger wanted to see his boss, shook his head from side to side and sighed.

'Too busy, *señor*, too—'

That was as far as he got before Emerson stepped by him and reached for the door handle. The deputy leapt to his feet with a curse which died on his lips when the tall gringo clapped right hand to gun butt and fixed him with a cold eye.

That was all he had to do. Suddenly ashen and shaking, the deputy offered a sickly smile and actually opened the door for him. Emerson nodded and went inside. He knew he'd been ready to use the gun. His fuse was burning short.

Sheriff Esquipulas was fat and ugly and sat slumped behind a huge desk. He appeared resentful of the intrusion initially but Emerson commanded his full attention when he loudly slapped the handle of the big .45 in its holster and stared him squarely in the eye.

The law turned pale and spread soft-palmed hands wide to show he really meant no offence.

'OK then,' Emerson drawled after both were seated across a desk liberally decorated by carvings of naked females. Tersely, he proceeded to inform the lawman of his movements and motivation over recent weeks. The man didn't interrupt until he mentioned the name, 'Calice.'

'*Señor*, I know this Calice,' he declared. 'I also know he has been in pursuit of this gang of which you speak. But you say he went off in a different direction?'

'We disagreed over different sets of tracks,' he lied. 'So, I followed one and he took the other. I don't know yet who was right.'

A short silence followed. Outside, a man cursed a mule he was handling and got soundly kicked for his trouble.

The sheriff appeared to hear nothing. 'Maybe I believe you, *señor*, maybe I do not. But I am a generous man so I shall not lock you up this time. Do you mean to be with us long?'

'Just as long as I have to.'

'Very well, you may remain – for a short time. But understand I shall be watching you.'

'Sure, sure,' he said, rising. The man irritated but he reminded himself he must keep out of trouble with the law in this strange place which was made all the more sinister by what he kept hearing of those vast and unexplored lands to the south. The huge 'Out There', as some ragged-assed citizens liked to call it.

He cleared his throat, was ready to go, but had one last question. 'You see any strangers around here recent – apart from me, that is?'

'This Ketchell you seek is not here, *señor*, of this I am certain.'

'Just what I expected you to say,' he muttered, going out.

He walked fast for a spell, scowling and concentrating. 'What now, Emerson? You've reached Reo

Leon and you're no closer to Ketchell than you were a week back,' he mused. 'So?' he said aloud. 'So, get on with it – that's the so!'

He proceeded to do just that, stopping by dive after dive to fire questions at conmen, derelicts, born losers, card-sharks, remittance men and whiskey-dreamers who could talk forever without once saying anything a man wanted to hear.

But at last, as he was nursing a double rye, the bartender he'd been quizzing suddenly snapped his fingers, and said, 'Hey, you're askin' about strangers – there was some here last night. I forgot.'

Jack made no response. He was suddenly played-out and fast losing interest – for tonight at least.

'Two men,' the barkeep insisted. 'They drank a heap and were throwin' their dinero around right freely.'

Emerson stirred and frowned. 'Money? Nobody has money here—'

'They got pretty drunk – them and the sheriff.'

He pricked his ears. 'They were drinking with him?'

'Uh-huh,' the man replied, then went on at his insistence to furnish a description of the two in question, but Emerson immediately lost interest on realizing neither could have been Ketchell.

So he downed his shot and ordered another. The gabby barkeep kept talking about his strangers for some reason, and Emerson had slid off his bar stool and was draining what was intended to be his final drink when he realized the fat man had switched from discussing drinkers to the subject of boots.

'Flashest damn boots I ever seen,' the man insisted when Emerson glanced sharply at him. He was a talker and loved an audience. 'Real damn fancy colours with these high heels . . . kinda spiky heels they was. And the way he was settin' you could tell he wanted everyone to see 'em and—'

He broke off as Emerson grabbed his arm. 'Two men you say?' he barked. 'And one with spike-heeled riding boots? Come on, let's hear everything – what they looked like, what they were wearing – everything!'

The bartender obliged readily enough and within minutes Emerson had heard enough about those distinctive boots and their wearer to be as good as certain he knew that it had been Ketchell and Danny in this fetid little bar only the night before. Blain and Danny – disguised as *vaqueros*!

His mind racing, he bought another round of drinks, tipped the bartender generously and kept him talking until the man mentioned horses.

'They talked about horses?' he cut in.

'Sure did. Come to think of it, most of the time they talked about horses. They was going to see if they could sign on for some big drive. Hope they do, sure were nice fellers – hey, what's this?'

'It's getting-drunk money is what,' Jack called back, heading for the door.

'Stranger and stranger,' the bartender sighed, smiling as he scooped up the notes.

'Who, Mitch?' a gin-ruined wreck slurred.

'Folks who show up here from time to time,' he replied, counting the notes a second time. 'OK, *amigos*, drinks on the feller who just left us. Wonder where he was goin' in such a hurry. . . ?'

Emerson was already there . . . namely at the mud-walled, semi-enclosed yard on the edge of town where a pair of half-dozing mules stood tethered beneath a gaunt joshua tree. Crossing the yard he entered the huge stables where he found the windowless gloom within almost impenetrable for the first few moments.

'Hey!' he yelled, halting until he could see more clearly.

He slowly realized how silent it was, and no hostler answered his shout. He was able to see just a little now as he went swiftly by a row of stalls.

'Where in hell is he?' he panted. 'Hey, Abe!'

He turned a corner in the stalls to see a dim light and the bulky shape of the stablekeeper seated upon a pile of corn bags, staring at him with his mouth hanging open.

'Judas, why didn't you answer?' he snapped, starting across. 'I'm in a hurry and—'

He broke off. The man was trembling and up close he saw that his eyes were wide with fear. Something wrong here! Instantly he made to whirl about, clawing for the six-gun at his hip.

A powerful figure loomed and a downswinging arm filled his vision before something exploded against his skull. He dimly saw the earthern floor rushing up at him then knew nothing.

CHAPTER 8

HELL TOWN

It felt as if he'd been submerged underwater and was now rising slowly from the green depths. Half-drowning, spluttering, he fought his way up blindly until he jolted back to full consciousness, still groggy and vision-impaired maybe, yet with every second seeming to thin that evil grey fog until at last he was sucking down sweet, clear air and somehow struggled to some kind of safety.

It was a long time before he was able to sit up.

He shook his head violently. Something clicked audibly in his head and the last of his double vision cleared, leaving him able to rise to one knee. Pain jolted through his skull, and when he explored his head with unsteady fingers they came away sticky with blood.

Someone had clubbed him – sons of bitches – and the water he'd thought was drowning him had been purely imaginary.

His first sharp awareness was of a familiar odour that was strong in the darkness, the smell of corn. Somehow he managed to rise to a half-crouching position, grunting from the effort.

'You are OK, *señor*?'

The disembodied voice startled him. 'Who the hell is that?' he demanded.

'José, *señor*.'

He identified the voice as the stable owner's. With a supreme act of will he heaved himself up to stand. For a time he swayed drunkenly yet managed to keep his footing while waiting for the spinning pain in his skull to subside. It was only then that he got to peer about in the deep gloom. Blinking and shaking his head he was eventually able to make out the vague silhouette of the man standing against the near wall.

'What happened? Who in hell hit me?' His voice sounded hoarse.

'I know him not, Señor Emerson. He came to the stables a short time before you arrive. He firstly looked at your horse, and then he pointed a gun at me and ordered me to be still and make no sound. This I did, and he hid in a stall until you came. I could not warn you of the danger.'

Jack swore and massaged his head.

'What did he look like?'

'Ahh, he was but young, not yet full grown. At first I mistook him for a *paisano*, but later when he was waiting for you he removed his hat. He was Americano.'

'What else about this son of a bitch?' Emerson demanded, suspicion beginning to knot his insides.

'He was dark with eyes the colour of midnight. A handsome man or boy, I would think. His movements were those of a cat, so smooth and swift.'

Emerson went totally still and felt something go cold within. It *had* to be Danny – that description fitted him to a T. Then came the ugly thought: surely if Danny could attack him that way then it had to be proof he was now beyond either his help or anyone else's. . . .

'Where are we?' he asked dully. 'Is this your corn bin we're in?'

'*Sí*. The young one dragged you inside here and locked it upon us. Unfortunately, it is a very sturdy room which I built that way in order that thieves would be unable to steal my grain. Now I cannot get out.'

'How long we been in here?'

'Perhaps a half-hour, possibly longer. That was a severe blow you suffered, *señor*.'

'Yeah,' grunted Jack. 'I know it.'

The only dim light in the room came from three air vents the size of dollar pieces drilled through the adobe ceiling high up. Seeing a little more clearly every minute now, Emerson considered his position. Plainly built to keep thieves out, the structure would do an equally good job of keeping somebody *in*. The walls were solid and the door two-inch-thick teak with iron hinges.

He swore. 'You tried hollering?' he demanded.

'At first, yes. But this building is too far distant from the street and I fear the sound does not carry far. A short time after we were locked in I think I hear gun . . . many guns, maybe. They cease after a time but since then nobody comes to the stables. It is very strange. . . .'

'Definitely not your best day, hero,' he rebuked himself bitterly, pacing to and fro.

'Pardon, *señor*?'

'Never mind. C'mon, we gotta raise enough ruckus so that somebody's just *got* to hear us.'

They proceeded to raise any amount of racket for a spell but without result and were exhausted by the time they finally slumped down in opposite corners. Yet they'd barely had time to catch their breath when they heard the voice. It was asking, 'Where are you, José?'

Emerson leapt to his feet and slammed the door with the heel of his hand. 'In here!' he roared at the top of his lungs. 'In the corn bin!'

A moment's silence was broken by the sound of quick footsteps. Then the voice again: 'José? You in there?'

'*Sí*. That is Rico, no?'

'Never mind the jawbone,' Emerson barked. 'Tell him how to get us out, damnit!'

'*Sí, sí*.' José bent close to the door and shouted, 'Rico, under the sawbuck by the lime kegs you will find another key.'

It seemed an eternity yet was in reality less than a minute before they heard the sound of a key grating in the lock. Next moment the door rolled back, light flooded in and two friends embraced as a grim-faced Americano strode out.

Jack headed directly for the stalls and was intensely relieved to find his black still safely there. He led the animal out and took it across to the saddle rack. It was as he reached for the saddle that he sighted the folded paper stuck beneath the cinch strap. With a frown, he snatched it up and opened it. The cryptic message scrawled with a lead bullet read, *Sorry Jack. It'll be all over by the time you get out. I'm in too deep to escape. It was all one huge mistake and I know I'll pay for it one day. My love to Sis.*

He shook his head. The note was both sad and final, yet there was in it also something he found immensely reassuring. He sensed Danny had come to realize the extent of the mess he'd been caught up in now. The tone of his note was regretful yet fatalistic.

But then the big question – where in hell had he gone? He stuffed the note into his shirt and got busy saddling up.

'*Señor*,' José panted at his elbow. 'Rico tells me that while we were imprisoned a bunch of *bandidos* stole the horses – the Ranger horses!'

'Figures,' Jack replied bitterly, waiting for his horse to release its pent-up breath as he tightened the girths, 'Anybody hurt?'

'I was not there.' Rico looked shame-faced. 'I lock my doors when I hear the guns. But Mañuel, he—'

'Was anybody hurt?' Emerson repeated.

'Mañuel say two Rangers are slain, some *vacqueros* wounded.' His face brightened. 'He also say *bandidos* die in the fight. So, this is good, no?'

Jack felt a quick stab of dread, proof if any were needed that he still very much cared one hell of a lot what happened Danny despite the attack or anything else.

He quickly finished strapping on his gear and scouted around for his Colt. He found it, holstered, then led the horse out into the yard.

José and Rico watched in silence as he submerged his head in the water trough, the water staining pink from the matted blood.

He dried himself roughly then hurled himself into the saddle without the stirrup. 'You know where Esquipulas is?' he barked.

Rico shook his head. 'No, but maybe the office. Mañuel say the sheriff was too late to stop the *bandidos.*'

'I bet he was,' Jack growled, and slapped the reins.

Riding swiftly from the yard he headed down a long and narrow alleyway to reach the square where he was forced to weave his way through groups of alarmed and excited citizens. Plainly the attack had jolted the whole lousy town into life.

He reined in sharply on reaching the abandoned cart where he made out the outlines of still bodies beneath canvas sheeting. When he jerked the cover off, two unfamiliar dead men stared sightlessly up at him, one of them a Ranger. He heaved a sigh of relief when he saw the other two lying upon the floorboards.

Neither was Danny.

'Esquipulas inside?' he demanded, swinging down.

'*Sí, señor.*'

He jogged across to the jailhouse. The light was gone with gloom stealing swiftly over the town. The gang would have a big lead by this. He must hurry.

He found Esquipulas slumped at his desk, beaten up and defeated, all former bombast gone.

'What will I do?' the man quavered, looking up. 'What shall I do—'

'Pull yourself together, is what! What in hell happened?'

'They-they stole the wonderful horses. All of them!'

'I know that, damnit. How did it happen?'

'Nobody knows . . . suddenly everywhere there were men with guns shooting into the sky and shouting orders . . . the Rangers were gunned down, others shot also—'

'And where in hell were you—?' he began, but broke off. He didn't have time for talk, reckoned he could well guess the answer anyway. He headed for the doorway, paused.

'Get across to the telegraph and wire Ranger

headquarters in Austin about this. Send another to Will Calice at Ford City!' He paused to sleeve his mouth. 'Which way were they headed – west?'

'South-west, *sí* . . . that is the bad thing. . . .'

'Why so?'

'Out there—' He gestured south-west. 'Out there – the terrible ones. . . .'

'What are you mouthing about?'

'Out there is the cruel land, *señor*. The Staked Plains are endless in the heat and the dust, and out there are the Comanches, most savage Indians of all, yet but children compared with the Terrible Ones. . . .'

'What?' he barked. 'What are you rambling about now?'

The sheriff reached out and grabbed his shirt-front, eyes bulging with terror.

'*The Comancheros!*'

The name seemed to hang in the very air, and even Emerson was silenced momentarily. Even the word itself sounded evil, as well it might. For decades the world of towns and settlers to the north had heard whispers, rumours and grisly tales of some tribe or grouping known as the Comancheros who were said to dominate the vast and unknown desert lands and lived by plunder, murder and trade with the Comanche Indians.

They were painted as clever, cunning and totally merciless – yet Emerson had been almost prepared to regard them as just another myth until that moment.

Then came the jolting afterthought: if the Comancheros were not simply a myth, and if they were great traders as rumoured, might that not explain why Ketchell had gone south with his horse herd, possibly to trade with these vermin, if indeed they did exist?

Esquipulas broke the thick silence. 'I see you have heard of them, *señor.*'

'You could say that.'

He moved across to the doorway to stare out. The shock was slowly passing and the longer he considered all that had taken place the more eerily credible it all seemed. For when he thought of all Ketchell had done – his long ride south of the Rio recruiting riders – and now this hint of a possible connection with those known as Comancheros, the more the suspicion seemed to make some kind of sense. It was easy enough to imagine a set-up with a ruthless trader in Ketchell and an eager market for fine horseflesh: the Comancheros.

He could well figure just what a prize a herd of high-class horseflesh might mean to the Comancheros whose name meant literally, 'Those

Who Deal With The Comanches'. It would give them the power and the ability to . . . what? Spread north, maybe? Maybe strike at Texas itself? Sounded crazy, yet didn't everything seem that way out here so far and beyond the last outposts of civilization?

Suddenly his teeming thoughts cleared and he realized what must be done. There was still no rock-solid certainty the Comancheros existed, but neither was there any proof that they did not.

But what if this nagging uncertainty inside him should prove to have a basis – and those evil scum proved to be real and poised to acquire what might well be the finest horse herd in all Texas?

How dangerous would that make them should they achieve that goal?

Suddenly he was yelling orders and striding for the doors. He was ready to make a fool of himself should he be proved wrong about either what he already knew or what he might yet find out. The one thing he was suddenly rock-solid certain about was that he simply couldn't afford *not* to mount a pursuit; he could worry later about whatever fallout or repercussions might follow.

He confronted Esquipulas in the doorway. The man was grey from shock and fear, which Emerson totally ignored.

He ripped off a series of orders at the man. 'Get these wires away right now!' He then summarized: 'The one to Ford City is all-important. If Calice is still there, as he well could be, and if he sets out at once on hearing from you, there's an outside chance he might get to intercept Ketchell before he can link up with the Comancheros. Well? What are you waiting for, man?'

Esquipulas scuttled off and Jack was heading out the door when the deputy seized him by the arm.

'Señor Emerson, what do you do now?'

'I'm going after them. I'll try to catch up then keep them in sight until the Rangers show up.'

'But you dare not ride out there – not alone.'

Jack brushed the man aside and went lunging out. 'I dare all right, *hombre* – no choice!'

The deputy trailed him out on to the landing but by then Emerson was already well along the rutted street. The man saw him mount, swing the horse about and heel it away to break into an instant gallop, scattering towners, and not once glancing back as he dusted towards the open plain. He was – so the watching man believed – most likely riding directly to his death.

The deputy thought, 'If only we had the courage to form a posse and go after him . . . to ride with him. . . .' Yet he was chilled by that very idea and it was as if ice was forming in his blood cells as his lips formed that single evil word: *Comancheros!*

He swung inside. This protector of the people needed a drink.

CHAPTER 9

THE COMANCHERO

Danny tilted his hat forward against the glare of the setting sun.

To his right and stretching ahead, the stolen horse herd moved sluggishly across the plain, hoofs drumming loud upon the hardpan, dust clouds billowing in their wake.

He was riding left point, the man closest to him a hundred yards behind with the remainder of the riders spread widely at intervals in back of the mob.

Those riding drag were all but invisible through the choking dust, faces swathed in kerchiefs and serape. Out front of the drive rode Blain Ketchell setting the course for them, the same course they'd been following over a night and a day ever since quitting Reo Leon. Due west.

Danny glanced away from the mob but there was nothing beyond it to arrest the eye, nothing but endless broken plains studded by yellowed outcroppings of dead buffalo grass shimmering brassily in the late day.

He had never encountered anything as empty as these Staked Plains, nor so lonesome.

Sometimes a lobo wolf might howl in the middle of the night and, once in a while, straggling dots of game were glimpsed far out. The occasional buzzard flock circled high above, appearing then disappearing as they seemingly followed some mysterious pattern of their own. Somehow those devil birds only seemed to deepen the all-pervasive evil atmosphere of these vast plains.

He was aware of his horsemen growing increasingly nervous the deeper into the alien country they ventured. Yet for some reason he was not affected that way. The others appeared to fear that something or somebody might suddenly rise up out of the yellow dust to menace them, and their reaction only served to deepen his contempt for them all. He made no attempt to discover the reason behind their fear – if indeed one existed.

So he rode alone and kept his own silent counsel. Whenever he rested he had barely a word for any man, and this now included his brother.

Every hour since leaving Hudson the former easy friendship between the brothers had crumbled a little further until now he knew he felt something almost like hatred for the handsome, reckless man he'd chosen to ride with.

He'd realized almost from the beginning that he had made a great mistake . . . but what was to be done now?

So, as he had done countless times this past week, he thought of Carmel and Jack, understanding now that what he had seen as interference on their behalf had in reality been a desperate attempt to save him from making a huge and maybe irreversible mistake with his life.

So, wrapped in frustration, regret and anger, he travelled the great eternal plain, half-fearing that eventually his always uncertain anger might explode into blazing rage and maybe he would get himself killed. . . .

'Hey, Danny!'

He hipped around in the saddle at the rider's shout, realizing only now that the herd had halted. He'd been so lost in thought he'd not noticed. He waved back in acknowledgement then swung his mount around.

The desert twilights were brief. It was full dark before evening chow was ready with stars showing point by point in the sky.

Accepting a steaming plate of side meat and beans from the hairy cook, he toted it off to a squat boulder on the rim of the firelight to eat.

The food appeared tempting and he set about it with some relish, but as had been the case every day now he found he could only swallow a few mouthfuls before thrusting it away, with what little he'd already devoured lying like a lead weight in his guts.

He took out his Colt and began cleaning the piece, glancing occasionally across at the others who were huddled about in little knots with their food, constantly darting nervous glances at the surrounding darkness.

A sneer twisted his lips.

Then he sighted Blain and went still. His brother stood alone on the edge of the light, the red glow of his stogie casting a glow over his face.

There was about his older brother a look of expectancy which was evident in the tense lines of his body ... the cocked and listening attitude of the handsome head. Each time a sound came from the night he would stiffen a little, eyes probing the darkness intently before he relaxed to drag upon his cheroot.

But a short time later when Danny saw Blain turn sharply and clap hand to six-shooter as he stared out into the great nothingness, Danny realized his brother must be anticipating trouble. He wouldn't act so jittery otherwise.

Yet as before, nothing eventuated and he went back to watching the others for a spell longer. They were either standing or sitting in huddles now, plainly made jittery by Blain's manner.

Eventually, Danny flicked his butt away and strolled casually towards the nearest bunch. Catching Ramon's eye, he jerked his head at him and kept walking. The sound of boots behind told him the other was following and, glancing over his shoulder, he saw that the man's surly insolence appeared to have vanished since their dust-up outside Reo.

He halted in the half-dark and the other joined him.

'What is it, Señor Danny?'

'What's scaring the men?'

'*Quien es?*'

'You understand all right. You and the rest of your bunch have been running scared ever since we quit Reo Leon. You afeared of the law coming after us? Is that it?'

'No, not that, *señor*. . . .' He paused to glance over his shoulder and then back to Danny. 'It is not the law we fear, but the Comancheros.'

'Comancheros?' Danny was surprised. He had heard much of those vermin out here, about their cruelty and inhumanity and the rest, but wasn't aware this might be their territory.

'You reckon they might attack, is that it?'

'No, *señor*, not that. Miguel, from my own village, he is a very clever man and—'

'Make it short. What about him?'

'Well, Miguel believes that maybe Señor Ketchell must plan to sell these horses to the Comancheros. He says this could be the only reason for us being brought out here to this terrible and dangerous place.'

Danny stared blankly for a moment. He was disbelieving at first, a chill sensation spreading over him. Deal with the Comancheros? What white man would ever do that? Yet even in that moment a small inner voice reminded him of that night when they had been discussing the horse herd and Blain had looked at him in that strange way and said. '*I got me a market!*'

'Señor?' Ramon asked when he failed to respond.

'Get lost!' he growled.

The man scuttled away leaving Danny alone to stare out across the firelit circle at the dim shape of his brother, feeling as though his head was spinning like crazy.

Comancheros!

This could not possibly be right. The Comancheros were creatures rated even lower and more despicable than the Comanches themselves – vampires living off the blood of Texas . . . men whom even other killers and outlaws detested. And now they were suggesting his own brother might be connected to *them*?

But – maybe that was possible. For surely this journey had revealed qualities in his older brother he'd never been aware of before, his ruthlessness, a coldness at times that made him seem a total stranger, the feeling on occasions that they were miles apart and not even linked by blood. . . .

It was a searing moment that was slow to pass and by the time it was gone he realized what must be done. He simply could not allow a question of that dimension to go unanswered – he wouldn't sleep. He must find out the truth or lie from the only possible source.

For some reason he found himself checking out his six-gun before turning on his heel and walking off in the direction of his brother.

As Danny approached the small fire, Blain turned, grinned and lifted a hand in a lazy salute. It was only as he turned away that Danny saw that they were no longer alone in the desert gloom, that silently, like a part of the night itself, strange ghostlike figures in white robes were emerging from the gloom over by the horse remuda and moving silently towards them.

Slender, sinister-looking horsemen wearing big shell belts and holsters slung around supple hips.

Comancheros!

He'd glimpsed these vermin at great distance once or twice in his travels, but never up close. Until that moment.

He had halted with right hand clutching six-gun as the bunch drew closer to his brother. He saw that their attire glittered with silver ornaments glittering from sombrero and gunbelt. There was about each of the party of five a common preening arrogance of manner with depravity and cruelty marking every feature . . . savagery without honest manhood!

Blain approached one who appeared to be the leader. He was taller than his henchmen, around forty years of age with a face that was still and watchful with a wolf glitter about the eyes.

Blain was now actually shaking hands with this creature as Danny stood staring, his face pale and taut as if he might be ill. Like any other south-westerner he'd heard Comanchero stories, legends and atrocity tales concerning these little-known denizens of south-western Texas. Most of what he'd heard or read he'd dismissed with a shrug as sounding unlikely, but face to face with these men now he immediately understood their evil reputation.

Shaking his head slowly, he again focused on the man who was plainly the leader.

Despite the warmth of this vast night this one wore doeskin gloves, a habit of dandies who wished to protect the fineness and softness of their hands. It added the final touch of unpleasantness and effeminacy mingled with the almost tangible cruelty that made a man want to step back for fear of becoming contaminated.

None of which appeared to have the slightest effect upon Blain Ketchell who appeared totally at ease in this dog-wolf's company as they conversed together in American with underlying overtones of French or Spanish – it was difficult to tell which.

He sensed that his brother and the man someone had called Chade appeared to be on familiar terms when Blain smiled genially and asked loudly, 'So, how are matters, Escobar? All well, I hope?'

'Very well, Ketchell,' the man replied without any change of expression. 'I see you have brought me the horses . . . and right on time.'

'Uh-huh, just like I promised. So, how long now since we set up this plan between us, *amigo*? Must be six months since I saw you at Guardia last. Say, where is the big boss tonight, anyhow?'

The Comanchero angled his feral head towards the west.

'Merely a few miles back along this trail now. He sent me on ahead to ensure all was safe and as it should be. I see that this is so. He will appreciate this efficiency, for this is surely a great and successful event. He admires any man who does just as he promises. You said you could equip the Comanchero with the finest horses for our great raiding campaigns in the future – and I see you have been as good as your word.'

'Well, we made a bargain, your bossman Guardia and me. I told him I could produce the horses and and he agreed to meet my price. And that's how it stands.'

'Did you have difficulty in coming by them?'

While Ketchell provided a brief account of the violence at Reo Leon, the Comanchero named

Escobar surveyed both the camp and the men, eyes chill and glittering in the firelight. His gaze finally rested upon Danny standing tense and alone over by the fire. As though alarmed, the Comanchero's thin lips tightened and his hand moved close to his gun.

Ketchell noticed this and interrupted the conversation. 'What is it? '

'*That* one.' Escobar indicated Danny. 'Why does he stare at me so?'

Blain scowled across at his brother. 'Something bothering you, kid?'

'You are!' came the instant reply. Danny's voice was thick with outrage. 'I can't believe you'd actually trade with these animals! Scum that any man would shoot on sight like a diseased dog! With *them*? God damn it, Jack Emerson was right about you, Blain. You're no good ... just a low-down animal!'

The fire popped noisily in the sudden quiet that followed the outburst. Danny backed up a couple of paces, slim body tight with anger while the vaqueros eased backwards, sensing the explosiveness in the atmosphere. The Comanchero, Escobar, stood taut and angry-eyed before his henchmen whose hands hovered alertly over gun-butts. Blain Ketchell was staring across at his brother with his initial astonishment instantly giving way to the anger that flooded over his features, making him ugly.

'You damned fool!' he snarled. 'You got to be loco. Anybody would have to be to believe I'd take that sort of sass from anybody, especially a half-baked kid!'

'Half-baked or not,' came the heated reply, 'you know better than anybody what I can do with a six-shooter, Blain. So . . . I'm giving you one chance. Send these lice packing, or I will.'

'You could easy get yourself killed with that kind of talk – *kid*!'

'I know it,' Danny replied with icy calm, seemingly totally fearless in that moment. 'I know I can't take everybody, but I'll take plenty . . . maybe you first.'

Ketchell's features twisted savagely. But before he could retort, Escobar cut in.

'Who is this *idiota*, Ketchell? Silence his tongue or we shall!'

Enraged and out of control within mere moments, Blain Ketchell was envisioning the vast undertaking which he'd planned so skilfully in sudden danger of falling apart before his very eyes, all because of a fool kid with gunsmoke in his eyes.

And as the rage engulfed him completely, he

was actually thinking, 'The kid has served his purpose . . . he ain't needed any longer. . . .' He was a man who'd never allowed anyone to stand in his way, and it was far too late now to change his ways, even had he wanted.

With the glittering eyes of every Comanchero focused upon the brothers now, Ketchell moved several paces away from both a pale-faced Danny and the Comancheros. His eyes drilled at his brother. He appeared ready to kill – and was. Yet maybe not personally – not this time around, leastwise.

For he was the only man who knew who was *really* the faster!

'Escobar's men!' he roared. 'Take him down!'

All seemed astonished by this with the exception of his brother, for Danny knew the other feared his gunskill – and with good reason!

His Colt whipped up too fast for the eye to follow, belching death.

The first man he shot crashed on to his back with his gun still in its holster. Moving his target line fractionally he drilled another through the chest, the man reeling away without actually falling until Danny's .45 thundered again and the Comanchero collapsed as other guns chimed in to join the hellish roar.

Danny flung himself down full length upon the

bloodied earth and rolled violently before getting another shot away at the looming outline of a tall Comanchero. From off to the far right another .45 bellowed and the slug creased Danny's right arm, sending his smoking cutter spinning.

His brother!

Blain had actually tried to kill him. Maybe he shouldn't be shocked, yet he was. So much so that he was momentarily frozen and was waiting in resignation and horror for the bullet that would kill him, but instead heard the voice of Escobar booming out, laced full of authority.

'Don't kill him, Ketchell! That is an order!'

The world spun in Danny's vision then turned black as a wave of Comancheros flooded over him.

When he awoke it was to find himself strapped to the saddle of a horse again plodding across an endless plain under a brilliant moon.

His hands were tied, his head ached and he was in the hands of the Comancheros.

That was all he knew or needed to know. He'd heard all the stories of his captors' cruelty and spite. He'd killed and hurt them here and he fully believed they would see to it that he paid in full for this before they would grant him the blessed relief of death.

But there was one question he was forced to ask, the answer that he must know.

'Did Blain hand me over to you?' he managed to croak.

'Of course,' replied the dim rider he knew as Escobar. 'He seemed pleased to be getting rid of you, said you had become both a nuisance and a Judas.' The ugly killer smiled admiringly. 'He does not permit interference with his plans, your brother. He would make a good Comanchero.'

And sadly, bitterly, Danny finally knew this to be true.

He must have lost consciousness, for how long he had no way of knowing. When he came to, the cavalcade was still moving across the eternal plain but now he glimpsed a glow in the sky up ahead. Another few hundred yards and he could see it was the light of a dozen camp fires flaring upon the plain.

His head throbbed and he was having difficulty holding it up, so was but vaguely aware of the gnarled walls of the arroyo they were now passing through. The arroyo was wide and deep and Escobar soon wearied of taunting him, and pushed on ahead. The horses made hollow clopping sounds that bounced off the stone walls . . . sounds that mingled with but could not drown, the sudden imperious order that was shouted from somewhere directly above.

'Reach – you sons of bitches!'

Up front, Escobar sawed his horse to a halt with a vicious curse as the others drew up sharply behind him. Through a gap between large boulders on the cliff rims above could be seen the dim silhouette of a man's head and shoulders with a rifle barrel gleaming menacingly in the gloom as it angled down to threaten every rider.

But was it friend or foe?

CHAPTER 10

STAKED PLAINS SUNDOWN

'*Reach you bastards – or die!*'

Again the harsh command roared out and Danny Ketchell felt a swift ripple of hope jolt through his aching body. For there was something very familiar about that voice, distorted though it was by the walls of the echoing arroyo.

Close by a pair of Comanchero killers waited for a response from the leader Escobar, who sat rigid in the saddle with glittering snake-eyes probing the shadows above. Slowly, almost impercebtibly, the killer's right hand crept towards his gun handle as he softly hissed a command.

'Kill him!'

A rifle crashed deafeningly and gunflame flared in the inky dark as Comanchero hands filled with guns and the racketing roar of shots and red flashes of gunfire ripped the night apart.

Danny struggled with his plunging mount as another animal went down screaming close by, the rider leaping clear.

The ugly thud of slugs slamming into living human flesh sounded close by and a tall man reeled, screamed and then fell.

By this, Escobar had both Colts out and blazing, ignoring the wild panic of the mount beneath him. The lethal figure behind the boulders above was blasting the Comancheros with twin handguns that bellowed and flared orange and wicked in the half-light, the gun crashes bellowing insanely loud.

Comancheros who'd been unhorsed were falling dead across the bodies of a riddled henchman as Danny kicked hard against horsehide to send his cayuse plunging forwards before it cannoned blindly into Escobar.

The brutal impact sent the Comanchero spinning from the saddle as Danny's mount slipped and crashed headlong. With his legs tied beneath the animal's belly he was unable to kick free. He waited for the expected pain of his legs being crushed underneath the beast's weight but a boulder took the full impact of the animal, saving his leg but slamming him into the ground hard upon one shoulder, causing him to howl in pain.

As his mount struggled to regain its footing he glimpsed Escobar some distance away down in a low crouch and triggering furiously with a bucking pistol in each fist. A moment later the man's head suddenly snapped back and he straightened up slowly with both smoking Colts falling from lifeless hands. Reaching full height, he shuddered once then crashed down headlong, never to move again.

Still dazed from his brutal fall, Danny felt his mount kicking its way back to its feet just as a clawing hand snaked out from the darkness and seized his reins.

'Danny!'

He stared disbelievingly into the face of Jack Emerson before slumping unconscious across the horse's sweating neck.

Two men galloped swiftly into the north-east.

The climbing sun shone in their faces and flung the shadows of their horses far behind them.

Spreading vastly on all sides in the early light, the Staked Plains emerged naked and hostile in the early morning glow.

And well behind them still, yet with their hoof-lifted dust clouds rising ominously into a clear blue sky, came the Comancheros, hammering furiously in pursuit.

'How you feel, Danny?'

'Fine,' came the panting response.

'I doubt that,' Emerson grinned.

'It's a fact,' Danny insisted, glancing down at the arm bloodied during the clash which the other had carefully bandaged then strapped against his body. 'I can scarce feel it now. That brandy and coffee we had back yonder sure was powerful medicine.'

'We might get to have some more of the same before we're through' – Jack paused to glance behind – 'if we're lucky. . . .'

Danny paled a little as he snatched a glance backtrail at what surely had to be as fearsome a sight as any man might see any place – howling, half-visible riders lashing foaming horses after them in headlong pursuit. 'I only wish we knew for sure if that's Blain or just the Comancheros on our tail – not that it makes one hell of a difference, I guess.'

'It's my hunch it could be both . . . they've both got plenty of scores to settle with us.'

'If you hadn't shown when you did the Comancheros would be settling scores with me already, I reckon. I've got the feeling that Escobar had some special entertainment lined up for me, all the trouble I caused that sonova.'

He paused a moment to test the pain across his shoulders and back, then shouted. 'You still haven't said how you just happened to show up when you did.'

'I didn't just happen by,' Emerson hollered back. 'I'd trailed the horses all the way from Reo. I caught up with you by chance yesterday afternoon, then hung well back into the dusk until after dark and moved in fast closer then. But I soon figured that all I could do for the time being was to keep on dogging the herd until maybe Calice showed, or even someone friendly. There was no point in taking on that bunch with you.'

'You saw the gunfight?'

'Uh-huh. But it was all over before I could make a move.' He spat and sleeved his lips and studied Danny's profile. 'You know, you sure as hell throw mean lead.'

Danny shrugged and glanced at his arm. 'Not

any more, I don't.'

'That arm will heal, boy. Take my word on that.'

'Yeah, maybe. But after what happened it sure won't be any good for fast drawing.'

'Well, there's more important things in life than pitching lead.'

Suddenly they were racing over rising ground that muffled hoofbeats and made shouted words easier to hear and understand.

'Could be I've already found that out, Jack,' Danny called 'But what happened after the dust-up in the camp?'

'Well, from then on it was almost simple. When those hardcases left with you I went on ahead. I hadn't gone far when I sighted the lights coming from the Comancheros' camp. That didn't give me much time to waste so I lay up in that arroyo, and just waited. They were fools to make a fight of it; I had the dead drop on them.'

'It was still a big risk you took. And I still can't figure why you did it. I mean . . . after everything that happened, and all. You might have just stood back and let them carve me up. I sure had it coming.'

'You're my friend, Danny, that's why.'

The simple statement hit Danny hard, seeming to him all the more remarkable to him in the wake of Blain's treachery.

'Jack—'

'Save it!' the other broke in. 'You're going to need every ounce of wind you've got before we're out of this. So don't waste any more breath talking, just make time.'

This they proceeded to do, galloping grimly through the burning day with horses labouring beneath them, the great stark plains shimmering on all sides and the horsemen behind them gaining inexorably with every mile.

They risked halting once at a tiny stream that snaked its lonesome way north to spell their mounts and snatch a quick mouthful of jerked meat washed down by cold coffee, then galloped on with their pursuers' fire falling dangerously close behind.

A desperate hour later they glanced backwards to glimpse riders at the base of their dust cloud, maybe a dozen or more. Jack figured that whoever it might be, Ketchell or Comanchero, their mounts would not have covered near as many miles as his black and Danny's sorrel had done in recent days.

It was an hour before sunset when they sighted the patina of rising dust off to the south-east. Scarcely daring to hope, they watched the billows swell and grow by the minute until there could be no further doubt. Only a squad of horses could raise a cloud like that.

They traded grim nods and urged drooping horses to one last heroic effort.

They imagined they were still holding their own, if not by much, when reality intruded in the shape of something that hummed overhead like an angry bee and they realized it was a bullet from behind!

Their pursuers had finally drawn within rifle range!

All too soon they were able to hip around in their saddles and differentiate between Ketchell's henchmen and the Comancheros. Emerson was even able to identify Blain's tall figure, his right arm rising and falling as he lashed his mount without mercy. Smoke puffed from a pursuer's weapon and the slug ricochetted off the ground ahead of the fleeing pair.

Moments later, Emerson's mount was struck, not mortally but enough to slow its pace. They slogged on for as far as they dared risk it before swinging in towards a cluster of heavy boulders scattered around at the base of a scrabbled ridge. As they reined in, Emerson loosed several shots to slow the enemy down before they dismounted and ducked for cover after slapping their horses' rumps to send them trotting out of the firing line.

No retreat now.

'Let 'em have it, Danny!'

Bullet chaos erupted fiercely as their first volley ripped into the oncoming rush to empty two saddles instantly. The reply fire came hot and close with bullets rebounding off rocks and screaming away in ricochets with a sound that ran down a man's spine like a buzz-saw.

Jack shot a rider dead with two slugs taking him squarely in the chest, Danny at his side blasting one-handed. Another rider tumbled from his saddle with his foot snagging in the stirrup and he was dragged away screaming as the unforgiving stones ripped him to pieces.

The attack appeared to be faltering a little until Ketchell's booming voice rose above the roar of guns:

'Charge 'em!'

They charged as ordered, but it failed and cost them dearly with more motionless shapes sprawled in the bloody grass by the time the surviving attackers were forced to break off.

The battle continued to rage for several further minutes before an enemy rider went loco and came charging in, yelling and shooting like a redskin out to count coup on a helpless settler.

The defenders brought down the fighting fool without difficulty, yet their faces were grim as they paused to reload. It looked bad and *was* bad for another dangerous slice of time – before Emerson suddenly stiffened at a sound. Hoofbeats behind them now? Impossible!

They whirled – and there it was. A Ranger troop came galloping in hard to go storming right on by the two defenders to engage a startled enemy that had been unable to sight them approaching from the west through the enormous pall of gunsmoke shrouding the battle site.

As the last Ranger thundered past, Emerson and Danny stood side by side staring after them to watch them close in swiftly on the outlaws who were now riding hands and heels in full flight from a superior force that seemed determined to run every last man down even if it took them all the way to the border.

In time it proved to be yet another triumph for the rugged Texas Rangers when the remnants of the once powerful gang of rogues, thieves and bloody murderers became trapped in a draw and were dealt with summarily and with the same degree of mercy as they'd shown those over whom they themselves had so often and murderously triumphed – the last man to die on a militiaman's bayonet later identified as Blain Ketchell.

And it was over.

Jack and Danny lay sprawled out side by side in the shade of a mighty cottonwood upon the gentle slopes of the Sangre de Cristos. It was cool in the dappled shade just sipping coffee and listening to the cicadas' drowsy buzz. It was five days since the murderous final battle out on the Staked Plains, already far behind them both geographically and in their thoughts.

Naturally there was sadness still that would linger for some time. Yet even now as they travelled leisurely homewards it seemed the whole bloody saga was slipping from their minds to be replaced by visions of home and how it would be when they got there.

Emerson tossed out the dregs of his coffee and stood up.

'Time to move out, Danny.'

'Yeah, guess so.' Danny sat up and adjusted the sling holding his injured arm. 'You know, Jack, I can't help thinking it was still pretty white of Calice to grant me a clean bill of health after all that happened.'

'Mebbe,' Jack grinned, raking fingers through yellow hair before donning his Stetson. 'But he was feeling pretty chipper when I put that proposal to him. After all, he'd just seen off the Blain Ketchell bunch, wiped out a whole mess of Comancheros, retrieved a mob of blood horses for the Texas Rangers, then even found the bulk of the Hudson Bank robbery in Blain's saddle-bags. Not a bad day's work, even for cocky Calice.'

Danny got to his feet and moved for his mount. He paused to stare back over the sweeping panorama of country far below where the lush green slopes surrounding them reached far back to merge eventually with the distant fringes of the mighty Staked Plains. 'It really is all over now, Jack. Isn't it?'

'If it's not it's sure on its last legs,' Jack drawled, sensing the younger man was saying farewell to it all . . . goodbye to the past . . . goodbye to brother Blair . . . farewell to the sinister and dangerous south-western lands that had so nearly claimed them both. Goodbye. . . .

After a minute Jack unhitched his mount and swung up.

'Let's put some miles behind us, Danny,' he grinned. 'I know at least one person back home who's going to be tolerably pleased to see us walk through the front door.'

Danny laughed aloud for the first time since the

last gunfight and, fitting boot to stirrup, mounted up. With the sun at their backs, they headed for home.